The Lake

The Lake
Tess Driver

The Lake
ISBN Paperback 978-1-7610990-3-8
ISBN ebook 978-0-9586825-7-2
Copyright © text Tess Driver 2025
Cover image: Anonymous photo courtesy of Pexels

First published 2025 by
GINNINDERRA PRESS
PO Box 2 Bentleigh 3204
ginninderrapress.com.au

'After all everybody, that is, everybody who writes is interested in living inside themselves in order to tell what is inside themselves. That is why writers have to have two countries, the one where they belong and the one in which they really live. The second one is romantic, it is separate from themselves, it is not real but it is really there'

Gertrude Stein, Paris

*For my daughter
Samantha*

CHAPTER 1

It is April 1997 and we are going back to the past, back to Rhode Island where you and I lived by Bonneville Lake after years of wandering. Jammed between Connecticut and Massachusetts, it is the smallest state in the USA. Unless a person knows about the America's Cup yacht race, historically held in Newport (which is in Rhode Island), they could be forgiven for never having heard of the place.

I became familiar with names like Narragansett, Buzzards Bay, Chepachet, Pawtucket, Escoheag, Pascoag, Situate, Woonsocket, and drove on Routes Interstate 95 and 495 regularly, using six-lane highways where interstate transports thundered. Rhode Island, a place of quahogs, manufacturing mills, enormous retail outlets and a decaying downtown, a place to pass through in half an hour, unaware that it is the most densely populated state in the Union. Just a tiny blob on the north-east coast, clinging to the edge of an enormous country. I told you that I often felt like that, clinging to the edge.

That is why the lake was such a special place. We lived apart from the rest of the world, the only ones, most times, swimming and sailing on the water. It was a two-mile walk to the local centre of Greenville. I walked there with our baby in the stroller to the AMP supermarket, the hardware store, the liquor shop, and sometimes stopped for a regular coffee at the coffee shop on the corner. See, I am falling back into using the version of English that I learned, to make myself understood!

A pusher became a stroller, the footpath became the sidewalk, my jumper became my sweater, the garbage became the trash, a white coffee become a regular coffee, petrol became gas, the postie became the mailman, pounds and shillings become dollars, dimes and nickels, lollies became candy, cockles became quahogs, the car bonnet became the hood, the car boot became the trunk.

There were no butchers or greengrocers, I bought everything from the supermarket. In the late sixties, you were earning about one hundred and sixty dollars a week, or ten thousand US a year. I was earning ninety dollars a week. Seventy dollars US fed us, clothed us, paid for the petrol and left enough for the occasional New York sirloin and a dozen donuts (apple cinnamon were your favourite, I liked coffee pecan). We heated them for breakfast on Sunday mornings, and with strong mugs of black coffee and the *New York Times* we would climb back into bed. The thought of New York was exhilarating and exciting. I found the reality disappointing. Expensive, dirty and hostile.

I learned to make French toast with crisp bacon and maple syrup. I learned to bake ham covered with maple syrup. I love the American sweet tooth and still cook so many American recipes. We ate hamburgers with baked beans and maple syrup, pancakes with maple syrup, bacon and eggs with maple syrup, banana muffins and maple syrup, corn muffins and maple syrup. No one seems to make tomato jello in Australia and I need it for my special hot chicken salad recipe. I have so many recipes collecting dust in the cupboard.

Within ten minutes, we would be out on Smith Street, onto the ugly commercial strip where traffic belched and roared past Dunkin Donuts and Howard Johnsons into downtown Providence, the Capital of Rhode Island. We lived on the edge of the lake in our quiet, secure home.

Thirty years ago, we moved into our cottage by the lake when the leaves were turning colour and the days were becoming shorter and colder. Ice was beginning to form on the lake in patches. In the setting sun, the leafless trees turned burnished silhouettes against the forming white ice on the lake.

Bonneville was a very large man-made lake for a textile mill that had ceased operation long ago. The mill was now only a vague memory in most local residents' minds; the huge, dark structure now stored furniture and antiques. I loved wandering around the cavernous, hollow building with thick planked wooden floors, hunting out a 'special bargain', like a child's rocking chair, old picture frames, gardening tools, and the tall cat, carved in Oregon wood, that held the fire tongs, shovel and poker. Its orange stone eyes glinted when the fire was lit. There was something very ancient about those orange eyes, almost mystical. I found that it had been carved by an Indian on the north-west coast in the state of Washington. I would sit and watch it, feeling sure that it had a spirit which was watching inside me, not a hostile knowing, but a wisdom that was comforting.

You were excited at the thought of learning to skate when the whole lake froze over. 'Our own open skating rink, just like Rockefeller Centre in New York.' You remembered the music blaring and skaters racing round and round, anticlockwise. I remembered the jazzy lace-up skating boots, the short skirts swirling and pink furry hats on long, blonde hair. Not for me. The inky water began to look so very cold and menacing. I remember you standing on the deck looking serious and thin in your white ski jumper with brown and green stripes, feeding the ducks. Probably for the last time before they flew away to a warmer place.

You learned to skate on the lake when it froze, pulling our baby's toboggan with her wrapped like an Eskimo in a pink fleecy suit and hood. Men made holes in the ice and sat fishing. They looked huge and bulky sitting on tiny stools with their lines thrown into cold, dark water that stretched below. Aspens surrounded the lake and the few houses built around the edges couldn't be seen because of the thick hedge created by the trees.

After the harsh winter of Rhode Island, when snow piled up to the window ledges, everything suddenly burst into flower by the lake. We were drawn back like the ducks that returned each season. The ducks came to the door with their babies to be fed, waddling between the sweet smelling lily-of-the-valley that blossomed every North American spring under the aspen trees. Their buds seemed pale, fragile.

Your brother decided to come down from Canada to America to study, so needed to apply for permanent alien citizenship shortly after ours was granted. He found work in a bar on the college campus. It was strange that after so many years, you and he should be living on opposite sides of a lake in Rhode Island. Three permanent aliens, we lived on the shores of Bonneville Lake. He walked over from the other side of the frozen lake with a jug of eggnog and a new girlfriend to celebrate with you when our baby was born in the Rhode Island Lying-In Hospital.

Hugh is artistic, flamboyant, loves beautiful women and old cars. You and he are like chalk and cheese. He's older than you, but a stranger would never know that. In the sixties, he was specialising in Theatre in Education, a very different area of study untouched in Australia. You are the serious one, so very loyal, always weighing the pros and cons and knowing exactly what you want. That is what I love about you. We balance each other because we are also very different. I balance on the edge of the lake, risking, defying fate. You have the boat there, or the bridge built, to save me from drowning.

We saw very little of Hugh, really, but he always turned up, seeming to sense when there was a problem, then would disappear. Always protective, unpredictable and generous when he was there. He became involved with a wealthy woman in New York. They lived very separate lives which crossed rarely.

CHAPTER 2

The Rhode Island Lying-In Hospital is not there anymore, it has been closed, but that's where Emma spent the first two months of her life as an American/Australian citizen.

'She's got a two per cent chance of survival,' warned Dr Gordon. 'She's ten weeks premature and only 2.4 pounds.'

I spent weeks looking at the tiny creature in the crib in intensive care, singing soft songs, showing her colours, shapes and reading stories. Always looking. Never allowed to touch. Sitting hours beside her while she struggled to breathe, hooked to wires and machines, her body almost transparent, her heart dark and beating. My first living baby, clinging tenaciously to life. After twenty-one days, I held my baby.

You said that she fitted between my wrist and my elbow.

I had given birth to a living person. That was a thrilling realisation when I held our fragile child for the first time. Suddenly, we were responsible for another life. I found that reality frightening. It had been a terrible time, that pregnancy, as I had threatened to miscarry again and again.

'You have to go on hormones,' Dr Gordon had warned, 'or you'll lose this baby. You've already lost two.'

Both miscarriages had been advanced and horrible and I was desperate to save this pregnancy. So was he. The drug, Diethyl Stilboestrol, DES, was being used in America with success for some threatened miscarriages. We never thought of side effects in the sixties; it was the era of 'miracles'.

'Anything, I'll take anything,' I begged.

What a two-edged sword. Years later, the fear of cervical cancer emerged to haunt the daughters whose mothers regarded the drug with reverence. I have my beautiful daughter, but at what price and what guilt.

You had to go into work in downtown Providence to Canal Street every day. Your job was hard enough, having to come to terms with the American way of doing things and establishing relationships with men who had not met an Australian before. Your wicked sense of humour met with blank unamused responses. I could not load you with my own fear and anguish. Your eyes told me that you knew.

I had begun to bleed again on 15 December 1968. It was early winter and we had tyres with studs. The trees were sprinkled with white, the paths had a thin crunchy layer of white, the first fall of winter snow. Once again, it was a trip to the Lying-In Hospital over frozen roads. You left me lying in a sterile white bed, I was only half aware that you had gone. They had drugged me, but I could smell their panic. The medical staff were preparing me for an emergency Caesarean operation.

There was no movement from the baby I was carrying inside.

'I'm afraid the baby is dead.' Dr Gordon's large face was so very sad as he bent over me.

You were standing at the end of the bed and I can still see the tears that filled your eyes. You quickly wiped the back of your hand across your face but when I felt for your fingers they were wet and shaking.

As I lay waiting for the pre-med to take effect, utterly empty, I felt a wrench in my gut. I screamed at the sister, 'It moved. The baby moved!'

'No, dear, the baby is dead.'

I was suddenly focused. 'You're wrong. The baby moved. Get Dr Gordon. Quick. Something is happening!'

She felt the swelling mound of my belly, 'My God, quick, get him! Get him fast!'

That is the last I remember until I heard a faint cry and registered the nurses rushing past with a minute bundle. My abdomen was dull and pounding. I felt you standing there, holding my hand hard.

You were grey and strained. My gut was burning, having been cut from the navel straight down.

'He saved you both but our daughter may die. She's tiny, too tiny to survive they say.'

Our eyes locked in grief. Such awful pain.

'But we have each other, they say you will recover.'

Days, nights, days, nights, weeks passed. Would she be blind, our child, if she did survive? Would she be mentally affected? (It was all possible.) Two days before Christmas 1968, I was allowed to leave hospital. You and Hugh picked me up and drove me to Newport, to see what the mansions and boats looked liked when sprinkled with snow. Great trees were stripped and fanning white like mad women's lace. There were no seabirds. The silence and the cold made me feel cleaner, purer inside, but you and Hugh were worried by my silence and sad eyes. I had been wrung out and left empty. I had left our baby behind in the hospital. You both were anxious about taking me to the lake, to an empty house, where the mobile hung motionless above the crib waiting for a baby to lie in it.

It was cold outside the hospital where I had been closeted in the warmth and routine for weeks. Suddenly the air hit me, turning noses and cheeks red. I could see my cold breath. You had a fire ready to light when we got back from Newport. As we opened the door to the quiet and chill, despite the heating, I smiled. You had found a fir tree and had decorated it with tinsel and lights. It stood in the corner, welcoming, with an erratic, coloured blinking.

The three of us sat by the roaring fire, toasted absent baby and friends. The world became warm and mellow as the mulled wine. You treated me like something fragile, wanting to feed me chocolates and pumpkin pie because I looked drawn, thin and white. We missed our families dreadfully.

CHAPTER 3

Christmas Eve, when the snow was falling and the lake was frozen, Dr Gordon called. 'She's a tough little character. I think she's going to make it. Enjoy your Christmas. You'll have her home soon.' Our eyes shone and we held each other very, very tightly.

'I knew it, I knew she'd be all right, I knew she'd survive.' How triumphant I sounded.

You were more cautious. 'Emma is still so tiny, there could still be problems.'

I didn't want to listen. It was as if the snow and ice had suddenly melted from the lake and it was blue and the sun was warm.

You had bought turkey legs and cooked them for Christmas lunch. They were the toughest, most awful things. I think you tried to grill them, but the Californian wine and the phone calls from Australia made the day wonderful.

Hugh was used to snowbound winters, snow chains and antifreeze for the car and digging out from snowdrifts. It was all new to us.

In February, after months of daily visits to the hospital, we were phoned by the doctor. 'You can come and take Emma home.'

It had been snowing outside, heavy, quiet and persistent. The radio warned of a blizzard. You were worried about driving in the snow with a baby who had spent almost three months her life sheltered in a hospital.

We knew nothing about babies, let alone our daughter who now only weighed five pounds; more than double her birth weight, but still so small!

We drove to the Lying-In Hospital. The snow had stopped and the sky was clear.

'It looks like the blizzard is not going to hit. It's probably safe,' you suggested.

The hospital seemed anxious that we take Emma. We were her parents after all. I could feel the nerves tingling down my spine as I held my child, knowing that she was now my responsibility. The hospital had done its job. She was sleeping peacefully as I held her and we walked to the car park with the bundle of clothes and equipment prepared by the nurses who had looked after their miracle baby. They had loved her dearly and were sorry to see her leave their protection and care. I could understand that and I could never repay them for what they had done, but she was our baby.

The sky was grey. I felt a flake of snow on my neck. The baby was suddenly heavy in my arms. I never smiled, like you, about snow, despite the moments of great beauty. When the sun came out before heavy storms had covered everything, it would make the silvery bark trunks shine and glow as if they had been polished. The shadows covered the ground in a long, spindly lattice. But that day, there was a stillness in the air, a sense of foreboding, that I always felt before a snowstorm.

By the time we were on Smith Street driving towards Ruffstone Road and the lake, it was sleeting with icy snow that made the car slide.

The world had become grey-white, full of swirling flakes of snow.

'Should we go back to the hospital?' I quivered.

'It's too far, it's set in.' Your face was set.

Friends were waiting at the door as we pulled into the cottage. The lake was covered in snow, everything was white as we crunched our way towards them. Old friends Howe and Emily had no idea we were bringing our baby home. They had brought us a kitten because they knew we had problems with mice in the basement. You called it Mouse.

It was minus twenty degrees outside and we were snowed in. There was nothing but snow. White fences, white cars, stark, white trees, white houses, yellow lights through windows. No road, no path, no shrubs, no bushes, everything white. No lake, no pontoon, a mass of snow falling, everything white. No birds broke the silence.

The sky was still heavy and threatening with charcoal clouds covering the patches of weak gold of a struggling sunset. There would be no sun falling into the lake in golden splendour for many more weeks. Even the trees, so tall and stoic, seemed bent and anxious. I had to believe that there would be a spring, a defiant burst of green as if the plants were calling, 'Ha, fooled you again!' Such resilience. It is appropriate that our daughter was born in a North American winter. She has the same resilient defiance.

The lights went out, the taps froze, the heating went off, the telephone was cut off. Four adults, a baby, a kitten called Mouse huddled around the open fire wrapped in blankets and sleeping bags. I defrosted snow to heat a bottle over the fire (the hospital had sent us home prepared) when Emma woke and began to cry. The nerves in my spine ran up and down like shorts in an electric cable, my head was thumping. I wanted my mother. I wanted to cry out, 'Help, I don't know what to do. My baby is crying and I don't know what to do except love her and feed her. Why is she crying? Is something wrong? Is she cold? Is she in pain?' But my mother was thousands of miles away where the sky was blue and the air was hot and the sea sparkled. Still it snowed as I held my baby tight, rocking in the rocking chair given to me by our neighbour Belle.

'Every Mom should have a rocking chair to soothe herself and her baby,' Belle had advised.

Oh, Belle, you were so right! I willed my baby not to sense my fear.

I had spent most of my life in a hot country where the temperature never fell below zero, where we longed for rain and cool nights, where winter meant a sweater and thick socks and umbrella. Even the winters in London had not been so cold. Grey, soggy and miserably foggy, but not below freezing like this, where everything outside the window was white and menacing.

I hate snow. It is quiet, cold and hostile. When a storm hits, you can see nothing but swirling white snow. The world becomes blind.

Humans are helpless if caught in it, people can freeze in their cars on the freeway if they break down. Any glow of light from a window anywhere makes one hold onto civilisation with a passion I never thought possible. The snow becomes so heavy on branches that they crack. You can hear the noise as they break and fall.

Suddenly, the kitten took off and ran up the curtains, hanging like a demonic thing, its eyes wild. You had stepped back and trod on it. Your feet in ski socks were longer than the cat.

'I'll go and check the furnace,' Howie offered, pulling on mittens, coat and a cap. 'The cat can come down with me.'

Howie Bradley was a stocky, dark-haired Rhode Islander. He and Emily had met at college and had married soon after graduation. Stubborn and strong, you could depend on Howie Bradley; he could tell ribald jokes for hours when the company was boring. Emily was willowy and blonde in comparison. She would look down and tut at her husband's jokes.

They seemed an odd pair, ill-matched. But what couple from the outside can be judged? Perhaps his love of fun, his smiling way of coping with things, was a balance for his wife's seriousness. Emily was a risk taker, had come from a wealthy, politically well-connected family. We never really knew about Howe. I had worked with Emily at the Elizabeth Jones Career and Fashion School in Providence, before I had become pregnant with Emma and we had remained good friends.

He picked up the trembling little kitten.

You were upset and suggested, 'I'll find some milk and soak some bread in it.'

Howie disappeared into the freezing basement with Mouse and the milk.

Emily boiled snow over the fire to make coffee, then she raced upstairs, insisting on changing the bed sheets. I sat glazed eyed by the fire, holding the baby, rocking back and forward, back and forward.

You went to bring in more wood.

'It's stopped snowing,' you announced, shaking snow off your shoulders, pulling off your jacket, kangaroo-fur mittens and your boots.

'The snowplough should be able to get through soon.'

But the snowplough couldn't get through. You and Howie decided to walk to Greenville to buy food. Emily said that everything would be OK and that I was a great Mom.

Howie got the shovel which we kept inside the front door in winter, pulled the door open and the freezing air gushed in. It seemed stupid, seeing a person sweat in the middle of the snow, but shovelling a path from the front door was hard work. He took one look at the cars. Great, unrecognisable mounds of snow.

'There's nothing glamorous about being snowed in,' he yelled at you when you were madly shovelling to scrape snow off the cars.

I agreed with him one hundred and ten per cent. We measured the snowfall by the feet of snow on the picnic table until it got too heavy and the snow collapsed.

Two days later, we heard the snowplough grinding down our narrow road. Howie and Emily would be able to dig their car out and return to Providence to open their restaurant. You and Emma, Mouse and I survived that winter. We can survive anything.

CHAPTER 4

In the spring, the road became slushy, the ice cracked and we no longer had to dig the car out of the snowdrifts. We no longer had snow piled up against the front door. The snow on the trees and bushes began to drip and overnight froze into icicles hanging like glinting decorations when the sun shone through them. Slowly, the snow disappeared and the aspen buds on the winter branches turned into pale green leaves.

One day, the tulip bulbs suddenly burst above the ground under the mailbox, the leaves appeared on the Dogwood and Rhododendron bushes. Everything was slushy and mushy underfoot. The lake turned blue with patches of snow and ice. The trees dripped as snow melted.

As the days became warmer, friends came visiting again to see the precious baby brought home in the blizzard and the mad cat who climbed the curtains and tried to run along the ceiling. When the soil became soft again, we dug and planted squash and rhubarb. I hung the washing out. It no longer froze, not like the first time I had hung out the shirts on a brilliant icy Spring day. The sky was blue, therefore the shirts would dry. I was desperate to wash things after winter, to smell sun in the clothes and watch them flap on a line outside. They hung like pegged, crucified torsos on a frozen line.

My neighbour, Kitty, laughed and shook her head. 'Lily, come and use my dryer. We never bother to hang things outside. I haven't seen anyone do that for years.'

Norma and her daughter, who lived further down just laughed.

The mailman told the story at the general store in Greenville. I became known as the lady by the lake with the frozen washing who sang her baby to sleep. 'She's Australian, you know,' I would hear when I pushed the stroller and my baby up to the village.

'How's the washing?' the woman in the coffee shop used to ask and I would laugh with her. Better to laugh with than be laughed at. She crocheted a granny Afghan for my baby. Now the dog sleeps on it in front of the television.

Even the girls in the AMP supermarket checkout smiled, and with their 'Have a nice day' would add, 'How's the washing?' 'It's fine, thank you,' I would grin.

'You're welcome,' they would add and smile at Emma lying in the stroller. Slowly, wisps of brownie blonde hair were covering her head.

She was a bright, happy baby. Dr Gordon wondered constantly at her alertness. Some people even drove up the dead end track by the lake after the thaw, to catch a look at the people from the other side of the world who had come to live among them.

'Don't worry,' Kitty confided. 'People here are not used to strangers, let alone people like you who have come from so far away.'

We are pulled back to the lake in Greenville, Rhode Island. It is where we became a family, where we made a home after our years of wandering, where our baby, Emma, learned to walk and where you were bitten by a chipmunk, remember? The mad cat was chasing the little squirrels with the bushy tails and, with your gentleness, you decided to save a chipmunk that had become the cat's plaything. It bit you hard. It was hanging off your finger with its long tooth right through your flesh and nail. You yelled in pain. You had to flick and flick to get it off. You eventually hurled the chipmunk into the lake, where its small, furry body floated for a time.

'It could have rabies, how would I know? We'll have to go to hospital, get it checked out.'

We were both shocked by the thought. Rabies! There were stories in the press about mad dogs down south foaming at the mouth and having to be shot. The injections given to anyone suspected of rabies infection were agonising. Straight into the stomach.

Frightened, we drove to the Rhode Island Hospital Outpatients, filled with the wounded and groaning, you holding your finger. The doctors were fascinated. They had never seen an Australian with a chipmunk bite and crowded round as you stood clutching that finger. They treated it with antiseptic, told us to monitor your temperature and thirst, but decided against doing anything else.

CHAPTER 5

Remember how we nearly lost Emma that first Spring? When the Lily-of-the-Valley flowered, mosquitoes also bred because they loved the lush green around the lake. I had put the baby outside in the pram to enjoy the lukewarm sun and had gone inside to do the washing in the basement. The neighbours gave us no warning. A small aircraft sprayed the area with Malathion to kill the mosquitoes.

I hadn't heard the spraying as I scrubbed shirt collars and soaked nappies in the basement. I had Joan Sutherland singing opera loud on the record player. When I came upstairs to hang out the washing, there was no particular smell in the air. I went to check on our baby and she was a chalky yellow colour, gasping for breath. When I picked her up, she projectile-vomited, wheezing and shuddering.

'Oh God, no! Oh please, no. What's wrong? What's happening?'

Kitty wasn't home, the neighbours further down the road weren't answering their door, I didn't have a car. I raced to the dead end of the road, where a boating journalist for the *New York Times* lived as a recluse. He was too drunk to drive me anywhere. Crying, trembling all over, terrified that I might have done something wrong, I phoned your office and you raced home.

'Don't die, please don't die, you are so precious.' All I could do was hug my child and try and feed her some boiled glucose water. She vomited everything. I paced up and down praying to a god I didn't believe existed. 'Please, I will do anything, just save her!' I had never felt so desperate or helpless.

We sped to the Lying-In, having notified them we were coming. Emma was still vomiting and gasping. She was yellow and pasty-looking.

'Spinal meningitis,' the men in white diagnosed. 'Go home. We'll notify you immediately of any change. There's no point in your staying here. We're so sorry.'

As we drove quiet and separate into Ruffstone Road, the air had become heavy and stinking. I had not smelled anything before in my panic over my baby.

'Bastards,' you roared. 'They've sprayed and didn't tell anyone!' Striding down the road, you screamed at Norma, the next neighbour by the lake, 'What have you done? What have you sprayed? Tell me, God damn you!'

She wouldn't say, refused to talk.

'Tell me now or I call the police. If my baby dies, it will be murder.' 'It's Malathion.' She wouldn't say more. Couldn't look at you.

'You bastards. Why didn't you say?'

Emma had been poisoned and her premature lungs couldn't cope. She was on the danger list once more. The nights were sleepless, we clung to each other, drowning in our pain. When the phone rang, we would leap to grab the receiver.

At last, the hospital. 'Emma is responding and will recover.'

'She has an iron will to live,' wondered Dr Gordon, and the psychologists at Brown University asked permission to run some tests with shapes, colours and sounds. They came and talked and played music to our child while she was struggling to live. When she was well, we continued going to the university, where the psychologists showed her more sophisticated objects and complex colour charts and movements with sound.

I picked a bunch of Lily-of–the-Valley and sat in the rocking chair, rocking, rocking. The cat sat on my lap, not purring, not moving. I still needed reminding we lived in a beautiful place.

Mac and Kitty were horrified. 'How could they do that to our precious baby?' They never spoke to Norma again.

We pretended the family did not exist and ignored them. We brought Emma home. This baby with the giant will to survive.

'She is amazing,' you said. 'We're lucky to have such a gutsy child, so very lucky.'

'We're lucky to have each other to cope with this,' I smiled.

'Without you, I could not have survived, I would have shattered. You have always been my quiet strength.'

Stubborn, determined, with a will of iron, it looked as if our daughter had inherited those characteristics.

I thought of the time we had mistakenly driven into the no-go zone around the Albanian border and how, with a James Bond cool, you had got us away from the border guards by offering them our towels. They had been fascinated by the towelling seat covers I had made for the Kombi. And the time we became lost in a gypsy camp in Bulgaria, that camp with the dancing bear, and the gypsies began to rock the car and try to pull us out. You didn't say a word but somehow, with stern looks, you managed to get us away with only minor damage to the car. That all seemed so long ago.

CHAPTER 6

In the summer, we borrowed a friend's Styrofoam sailboat and sailed on the lake, singing and drinking beer and having barbecues and making new curtains and holding lamington, pavlova, pie-and-pasty parties by the lake for our friends.

Tom and his girlfriend Rachelle had just moved to the State and rented a cottage further up the dead-end part of our road. They didn't know anyone in Rhode Island, so we thought we would introduce them to a few people whom we had met and liked. We couldn't see their house at all from the road or the lake, but we could see and hear his red boat. Rachelle was shy, a French Canadian primary school teacher, but Tom was a laughing, jovial, Spanish-looking textile salesman from New Mexico, a hail fellow well met, come-and-have-a-water-ski man, who offered everyone a boat ride and a beer and a ski at the party, and any time anyone wanted to visit, they would be welcome.

I was wary of Tom. He was too boisterous and overpowering and seemed to be insensitive to people and places. The lake was not a place for a ski boat, which was noisy and speeding. The life on the lake was placid and he introduced an unwanted element that disturbed the peace. Again, it was an incongruous coupling, he and Rachelle. She asked me to go to the gym with her, she was too shy to go alone, so Monday and Wednesday nights we would travel to Gardenvale gym, where Tom had done a deal for membership for us both.

Tom did deals for boats and memberships to gyms and golf clubs and typewriters and sewing machines and trips to Hawaii. He would just say, 'I can do a deal,' and suddenly the article would appear.

He wanted to do a deal with publishers for the work I had written on communication skills for a course at Elizabeth Jones Career and Fashion School. 'I can get thirty thou, no worries. They'll use it in schools. I've already got some principals lined up who want to buy it, all you got to do is sign.'

Tom was the first real hustler I had ever met. And, no, I didn't sign because one day, the boat was gone and the cottage was empty when I went to collect Rachelle for gym. They had disappeared as quickly as they had appeared and my manuscript for the communication skills programme had disappeared as well. It was the last I saw of it. All that work, gone.

CHAPTER 7

A canopy of feathery green covered the aspen trees. The lake turned silver. One summer, you and Ben bought a rowboat and piled everyone in it for a row around the lake. Tilly and Emma were at one end with you, Ben in the middle and two boys at the other end. You wore wide smiles and no life jackets. You all went fishing in the rowboat, Ben's three boys and you. Everywhere in the world, I have seen men and boys fishing. If all the world's leaders were taken fishing whenever there was a crisis, we might have peace.

Tilly and Ben would drive down from Massachusetts with their four children, who swam and splashed in the lake. We never thought of it as being anything but a safe place. Tilly and I would sit on the deck, sunbaking in our swimming costumes, drinking wine coolers, while you and Ben barbecued lunch and drank cold Budweiser beer out of stubbies. They had never cooked barbecues before.

We went with them in the summer to Cape Cod, a long, thin peninsula like an octopus tentacle curling into the Atlantic Ocean. In 1620, the Pilgrim Fathers had landed at Province Town, where in 1969 Ben's dad had a fishing shack. The fishermen's boats were surrounded by squawking gulls as fishermen pulled in their nets. Provincetown was mostly grey and white, the grey roofs steep-pitched to cope with the heavy snowfalls in winter, grey slatted wooden walls, white door frames and window frames. The houses were bordered with picket fences.

We turned brown in the summer sun and dug for quahogs as Emma began cutting teeth and eating mashed vegetables and chicken. I knew nothing about babies. Tilly taught me everything I needed to learn to look after my child.

On the long summer evenings, we sat on the screened porch and watched the water turn the colour of mother of pearl. I would sit with Emma on the rocking chair and she would chatter to the ducks as they came up quacking, bossy to be fed. We would rock together back and forth and I would sing to her, soft and silly songs. We were so very happy.

Mac and Kitty, our closest neighbours, watched our lives and smiled and they were also happy. Kitty stood behind the large picture window, always looking immaculate, untouched, perfectly groomed. They had never swum in the lake, or fished or picnicked, instead they watched us do those things.

Mac went to bars and in the winter we would dig his car out of the snow because he would go off into the snowy edges. He used to drink bourbon. You had to get him out of the car or he would freeze. He was heavy and fat with flushed cheeks and beautiful tweed jackets. We would have to drag him sometimes through the snow and Kitty would watch anxious through the picture window.

Kitty asked us to dinner to celebrate Emma's recovery from the poisoning (and I think to say thank you for helping Mac). We had never been further than the kitchen door, but sensed that there would be nothing out of place, like Kitty. We dressed carefully. I wore a white dress and Kitty cried, 'You are the most beautiful young couple!' Mac smiled. We were embarrassed but proud as we set the baby's basket by Mac's leather recliner.

'Sit down, children. What would you like to drink? Martini? Dry?'

Mac was shy and gruff. He had made his money from tyre-retreads, but in his retirement was at a loss to fill his days. They were both in their seventies and sometimes Kitty's daughter and grandchildren came to visit. They also never swam in the lake, but the small, round granddaughter, Sally, with her huge black eyes and shy smile, would come to our house and ask to hold Emma. She would sit in the rocking chair, gently rocking, holding Emma against her in her lap, and tell her long and involved stories.

The dining room table was highly polished mahogany, set with white starched Irish linen and heavy silver. The glassware shone. Everything gleamed with care and refinement. We asked them questions about Rhode Island, about their families, the business and the politics of the place. They were probably Republicans, but we didn't ask. We were the strangers and I remembered my mother's advice, 'A still tongue is a wise tongue.' Yes, for once in my life I remembered her advice. Kitty smiled and looked at Mac with great affection. This was a second marriage for both of them. We were not used to knowing people who had been divorced and remarried. In the sixties, divorce was still unacceptable in middle and working-class Australia.

They were not really interested where we were from and why we were there as neighbours. We were young people whom they had decided they liked. Kitty said, 'I like how you are, friendly and open.' She appeared bound by etiquette and expectations and was amazed that we had left our home, left our families behind and had wandered without worrying about money or security. Money and security were very important to Kitty and Mac. I wondered why.

You told me that I ask too many questions about everything. 'Just accept people as they are,' you warned.

Anyhow, one more dry Martini and I wouldn't be able to ask anybody anything.

I still cook the meal Kitty served. Chicken breasts, broccoli, cooked in chicken and wine sauce, hot rolls, salad, a bottle of Californian Riesling, Southern peaches. I will share this recipe because it is too good not to share. Enjoy!

Packet frozen raspberries

Packet frozen blackberries (with juice)

Blend and sieve 1/4 cup of sugar and 1/2 oz Southern Comfort

Mix all the above and stand for two hours.

About two hours before serving, add uncooked white peaches.

It all turns heavenly pink and your tastebuds will think that that is where you are.

We ate, we laughed, felt peaceful and loved. Emma slept. The ice on the lake melted.

CHAPTER 8

Our house was a second hand dealer's dream, compared to Kitty's house which was like an illustration from *American House and Gardens*. I made one set of curtains for each room. Our rugs and furniture covers did not change with the seasons. We did not hang any wallpaper. We had no colour theme. But our house was warm and comfortable, and it felt good.

You even bargained with the man in Sears for a better price for the sofa. I think he was so surprised that he agreed and included the delivery cost. It was probably the accent that confused him.

I had noticed that many people changed the decor of their houses come spring, after the long winter. You had removed our winter storm windows and stored them in the basement. I had replaced the wreath of holly and berries with a wreath of bright flowers. I painted the mailbox yellow, and played Stravinsky's *The Rites of Spring*, understanding the music for the first time. You had swept the slush from the enclosed porch facing the lake, I scrubbed away the last reminders of winter, as we prepared for the long summer evenings.

Emma began to walk, her second spring, and the ducks returned to the back door. You had skated with the sled in winter with the tiny figure wrapped in pink whizzing across the ice. No wonder she thought she could walk on the lake. My back was turned digging the vegetable patch when I heard a splash.

I had not realised that she had become so quickly mobile. Weighted down with a parka, thick pants and kangaroo fur boots sent from Australia by grandma, I never dreamed she would waddle down to the edge of the lake so quietly and quickly. She had seen the ducks and was off!

At the sound, I turned and ran to the lake. Em had walked off the pontoon and was floundering in freezing water. I tried to reach her. I laid down on the deck to pull her up over the edge, but the wet clothes were making her too heavy. She kept going under. I screamed. Geoff, an Australian friend, who was visiting from Boston, raced out from the cottage and helped me drag Emma out the water. We were both soaked and shaking. She was miserable and crying and coughing. Geoff wrapped us up in towels and rugs, built up the fire until it was red and hot, then poured me a brandy.

'Geoff, thank God you were here,' I stuttered as I rubbed the little body until she was glowing and warm after a hot bath.

'Here, get this into you. She's got a charmed life, this little one!' He was right.

I was still shaking. Emma had walked on icy water without success and had sunk straight down with her heavy clothing. So many years of her life used up in the first few years of existence! Shivering, tears, hugs, comforting kisses, we sat in the rocking chair by the fire, soothing and stroking.

I had watched this baby from one day old. Too delicate to touch but so tough inside. I had looked for months through the glass as she slept, wondering what dreams she was dreaming, how was she feeling, my breasts longing to feed her and my arms longing to hold her. My aching for her had dulled the physical pain of my own body.

When she was three months old, I had cradled the miniature, wrapped figure, caressed the toy-like fingers, wondered at the perfection of fingernails and ears and the delicate arc of eyebrows. My breasts had been so sore, they would never feed my child or know that intimate contact which is mother's and child's alone; never have they nuzzled a child nor felt its soft breath and touch against them.

'Emma fell into the lake today,' I mentioned when you arrived home from work.

'She what!'

'She walked into the water when my back was turned.'

You were speechless and I was grateful for that. The awful horror of it only hit you when she was tucked up asleep for the night clutching her blue rabbit. 'She could have drowned.'

'Yes.' I couldn't say more. 'But she didn't.'

We watched our child sleeping in the wooden carved crib, Belle's gift.

White curtains covered in elephants and laughing bears and giraffes moved in the breeze. Emma lay with blue bear on one side and Raggedy Anne on the other. Her favourite doll with red tousled cotton hair, beady eyes, red cheeks and lips, a doll who could be flung around, still smile and be cuddled again.

Raggedy Anne was a lifeless doll. My child was proving that she was not. She was alert and responsive and every movement was intelligent and focused. Her sight was perfect and her coordination unaffected by her premature birth. I would sit and talk to her as the mobile of suspended elephants on bicycles, cycled lazily in the air.

Sailing with Em on the lake, we had no idea that we were living dangerously. We splashed water and watched it glistening as it fell, we waved at birds and whistled and flapped our arms. We went to the sports equipment store to buy golf balls and saw small yellow water wings for water safety for infants.

We suddenly realised what risks we had been taking and bought them immediately and though even the smallest pair was too big, we fitted them together across her shoulders for protection. We were new parents and totally naive about the dangers confronting a small child.

The three of us together on the water were close and happy. We put the horrors behind us, basking in the joy of the present and did not think too much about the future.

CHAPTER 9

There were strange things that happened by the lake. It feels as if it all happened yesterday and I cannot believe so much time has passed. I think of the house by the lake as I am bent writing in an awkward seat on a stuffy aircraft that is my home for the next few hours, gliding solid through the dark. It is night, May 1997. All around me, people are breathing heavily or squirming in a restless sleep or reading. My mind is not here, the sounds are a background to my memories. I am at the lake. So often I have thought about our life there but never before have I felt that I must put it into writing. Suddenly I know that if I don't write about it now, it will never be written. I have to write about it for you because I think that in our long marriage, our years by the lake were our happiest and our saddest times. We were young and in love.

When we moved into the tiny stone house, built as a whimsy by a wealthy American, who loved Wordsworth and the cottages in the Lake District of England, it had been unoccupied for months. You expected the witch from *Hansel and Gretel* to emerge, broom and all. I can hear her call, 'Come in, children,' and we did. It was our storybook house.

The house by the lake is rough grey stone built like fitted jigsaw pieces with a steep roof of slate shingles. Turning into Ruffstone Road, I pass the public swimming area, pass Norma's house and there it is with the front door so close to the unsealed road. Small-paned windows are on either side of the front door, their frames and the door painted dark brown. Knock on the wolf's-head knocker and I enter, suddenly becoming aware of space. The house is lined with stained pine, a golden syrup colour that reflects the light. Two bedrooms are upstairs and a smaller room tucked under the eaves with a bathroom. I look over the balcony to the large area below dominated by a stone fireplace, big enough to sit in and the stone chimney, blackened by smoke, stretching up through the cathedral roof. I walk down the gingerbread carved balustrade into an area that is wide and welcoming. Paned windows look out onto the aspen trees and the lake. One door to the right leads to a tiny kitchen and the basement dug under the house. The furnace for the heating, the well and the washing machine are there. The door straight in front of the stairs leads to the enclosed porch, an outdoor room to sit and listen to the night and the lake sounds in summer. In good weather, I drove the car down the side of the house to the big door that led to the basement. (In winter, I could not see it. It was under snow.) Friends parked their cars down the side near the pontoon in summer.

'We are in a good area,' I wrote to assure our parents, who had been shocked by some of the places we had been. We sent photos of a large home that looked as if it had been transplanted from a Virginian plantation of a *Gone With the Wind* movie set. Soaring columns, enormous wooden doors, long windows and shutters, a sweeping drive, lawns gliding to the edge of the lake. Our cottage was a doll's house in comparison, but no one in Australia would know that. We said, 'This house is around the corner from our house.' It was, almost.

The things we had collected in our travels decorated the cottage. Coloured woven rugs from Portugal, Spain and Greece, copper pans and ladles from Turkey, old dentists' spoons from Denmark, reindeer pelts from Norway, all embedded with memories. The copper kettle was one of them. Every Spring, you bought me the first yellow daffodils. Somewhere, you had found flowers to fill it and had polished the kettle before you brought me home from hospital after Emma's birth. You had placed our gnome, our pipe-smoking Cornwall gnome, alongside it. 'He's for good luck,' you promised. We needed every bit of luck that he could bring at that time.

So many years ago, a lifetime ago, a different time, and yet it sits in my memory like yesterday. I can touch the stone walls in my mind, run my hands along the rough edges, rub the panelling until it glows, feel the warmth of the sun as we sit laughing in the boat, I can hear the ripples of the water, the wind in the aspen trees, the roar of logs in the fire, children laughing and splashing, smell the maple syrup and the bacon.

Safe, precious memories.

CHAPTER 10

A doctor, separated from his wife, had been living in the cottage when I saw it advertised for rent. He had a heart attack, fell down the stairs and had gone back to his wife. When we moved in, there were phone calls from odd sounding people looking for the stricken doctor. 'He's gone,' I'd say. 'We live here now and don't know where he is.' Kitty came across the road one day with a gift for the baby, a worn, engraved old silver christening mug. 'Oh, him,' she said, 'he's a Mafia doctor, checks the prostitutes, the Whites and the Blacks. There were two beautiful girls used to come to see him. The blonde came in a white Cadillac, dressed in white, white poodle always with her, wore white furs. Then there was another girl we used to call Blackie. Black Cadillac, tall, long black legs, red fingernails, carried a black poodle, wore black furs.' Kitty laughed. 'I think they both ended up in concrete in Rhode Island Sound. No wonder he had a heart attack.' Kitty saw everything through her large picture window.

We had the oddest collection of furniture in the cottage, wicker, covered boxes with decoupage, shop samples, borrowed baby furniture. Generosity. The wonderful generosity of Americans, their warmth, hospitality, we were welcomed and we observed everything, listening, often in silent amazement.

Samuel Bisquet was wealthy, a thirty-two-year-old millionaire from stock market investments and one of the most generous men I had ever met. We used to stay in his ski chalet before I had Emma. He gave us a set of keys and said, 'Anytime you want to ski, the lodge is yours.' The three-storeyed wooden chalet at Mt Snow overlooked the Vermont snow fields. Sometimes I think he said 'Use it' to everyone, because we shared bedrooms with characters who arrived anytime of the night.

That's how we met Uncle Rocco and Lisa Jean (LJ to her friends).

She taught you to ski fast and to skate while Rocco and I made snowmen. We used to pelt you with snowballs when you came in from a run. For a small wiry man, Uncle Rocco was strong and certain with his aim. You always looked surprised, standing there with your skis and stocks, quite defenceless.

The snow and ice scared me. I found it strange and menacing. Stuck on skis, you and LJ slithered your way around the snowfields of New England while Uncle Rocco and I sat by fires, read books and cooked (his mother and wife were Lebanese and he cooked Middle Eastern dishes with spices I had never heard of). He loved Miami and Florida and would move there except for business and family. He was retired from the restaurant business, he said, and I can still see him shaking his silver hair, his smiling olive face like an Arab hawker, when I told him our friends were going to open a restaurant.

'Are they prepared to pay ten per cent to the police or ten per cent to the racket for protection? That's the only way they'll stay open.' (They didn't listen to him and a bullet through the window and a fire finished the venture.) I often wondered which side Rocco had been on to keep his restaurant business flourishing. He lived in an old house on Federal Hill. Upstairs lived his wife and his son, who he supported. By living downstairs, he was able to see his boy, but that came at a price because when his wife was annoyed with Rocco, she banged her broom handle on the wooden floors to make sure that he rarely got a good night's sleep. She banged any hour of the night.

There were heavy brown rings under his eyes and he always looked sleepy. I had never met a man who had so many gold fillings; they flashed when he smiled and he smiled quietly, often. We wondered about him and LJ. She looked so normal, he had an air of danger. She was athletic, teased and laughed heartily. Rocco's guttural chuckle lit up his dark angular face; the grin was villainous and attractive. Her hair was brown and curly, his hair was smooth and silver. His hand-made leather winklepickers contrasted strangely with her ski boots and skates. He was years older than LJ, who looked like the flamboyant girl-next door with an hourglass figure. Such a strange coupling and yet they had been lovers for many years.

LJ introduced us to her friend Eleanor and Eleanor's lover, Connor. Both women were in the jewellery business and lived in Pawtucket, but Lisa Jean was involved in the manufacturing of jewellery from precious stones and gold. Connor was an important businessman in Rhode Island. I felt that Rocco would be good protection; he made me feel that he was not a man to be crossed. There was something sinister beneath his quiet and I could never work out why he gave me that feeling.

It was your boss who said that he had a friend who wanted to meet these Australians (in the sixties and early seventies, we were an oddity, not seen much on the east coast of America) and that is how we came to meet Sam Bisquet. They knew we had had a prime minister who had drowned swimming in the ocean and wanted to know where his security people had been. Tall, quiet, blond, Sam took us to meet his mom when he found from Lisa Jean and Rocco that we had no furniture, driving us down to Warwick in his silver Monaro to the huge, sprawling bungalow with lush green lawns and towering trees. It was the first time we had heard woodpeckers.

Belle was large, vague and very blonde and welcoming. 'Come in, children. Any friend of Sam's is a friend of mine. He says you're short of furniture. Come to the basement, I've a few things you might like.'

Every wall of the house was wallpapered, even the stairs to the basement. The wallpaper was changed with the seasons. The basement was an Aladdin's cave.

'Choose what you want. Samuel will have it delivered. I don't want it back. A Chinaman brings me in boats full of stuff.'

Next to Chinese porcelain, Philippine wicker, Thai carved chests and rolls of silk, Indonesian carved furniture jostled for display. We had stood, lost in our naivete.

'What do we do?' we muttered as we selected a modest collection of chairs, lamps, a table and at Belle's insistence added a few more pieces, a rocking chair, some side tables, a carved crib for the baby.

'That's better,' she crowed, smiling and happy.

How do you respond to such generosity? We sent flowers. We had boomerangs and Ugg boots sent from Australia.

Years later, we heard from Uncle Rocco and LJ that Sam was on the run in South America. He'd lost his money and was acting as a gigolo to wealthy women in Mexico. We were told he'd been having an affair with a woman whose husband was in gaol. On his release, Sam had had the husband beaten up. Now he himself was being hunted. We never heard what happened.

Things are never as they seem. That was the story of our life in America.

CHAPTER 11

When I first arrived in America, I felt separate, an observer, a cautious observer. We had arrived in 1966 near Thanksgiving, with tourist visas but with every intention of working. You had been offered a job with an engineering company in Rhode Island after they flew you from Canada for an interview in New York. We would need green cards and social security numbers but that would only happen if we were awarded permanent alien status. I liked the idea of being a permanent alien; it sounds so non-committal. You had been assured that there would be no problem. After all, Australians were allies of America and were fighting in Vietnam. We had six-month tourist visas for America and did not anticipate the hard time we would confront at the Niagara crossing between Canada and America.

It was the time of draft dodgers, young Americans escaping to Canada to avoid conscription into the army because of the Vietnam war. We hadn't stopped to think about that because we were going in the opposite direction. Borders between America and Canada were tightly controlled. 'Why are you coming to America?' The border guard eyed the hire car suspiciously and our cases piled in the back. He peered through the rear window, his belly rubbing against the boot of the Dodge. 'Passports. I want to see your passports. What are you doing?'

'We're coming to visit and stay with friends who live in Massachusetts,' you answered, handing the passports through the window.

He looked at the passports covered in stamps from every country in Europe where we had wandered and Greece, Bulgaria, Yugoslavia, Turkey. 'Where have you been staying in Canada?'

We didn't know the exact address, except that it had been Mont Royale in Montreal with your brother. You were probably too old to be drafted, but he looked at you suspiciously.

'What do you do?'

'I'm an engineer.'

'You're coming here to work.'

'No, to visit friends.'

'Who are they, where did you meet them?'

You couldn't say he's my new boss and that we'd never met them, so I lied.

'They're a couple we met in Greece. They asked us to look them up and stay if we came to the States. I phoned them from Canada. They're expecting us.'

It was only a half lie and I was feeling sick and frightened. We had never met anyone like this in all the borders we had crossed.

'Out of the car, both of you. Open the hood. Open the trunk.' He hit the hubcaps hard. 'Take out the cases. Open them.'

I was shaking with fury and fear, a dangerous combination. I hated this power-hungry, fat little official. I was feeling sick. I just knew that he was the type who would bite his fingernails down to the quick and as he fingered his way through my personal things, looking at me all the time, I knew I would have to wash everything to get his grubby feel out of them.

'Is this the way you treat your allies? Our country's fighting with you lot in Vietnam. Thanks for nothing!' It was out before I could stop it. There were tears in my eyes and I thought I might vomit over his shiny black lace-ups. Pregnancy does strange things to hormones and I knew that I was pregnant with morning sickness and tingling breasts.

Still surly and unfriendly, he went to a small office with our passports. When they were returned, he had reduced our six-month visas to two months.

Stunned, you muttered, 'What are we letting ourselves in for?'

'Welcome to the United States of America!'

I wanted to spit at the sign. 'You've got to be kidding?' I muttered.

Your American boss, Ben and his Scottish wife, Tilly, lived in Massachusetts, where they took us in as part of their large family, assuring us, 'Everything will be OK.' Their kindness enveloped us in a blanket of security when everything else was so uncertain.

After so many years of travelling, living in an attic flat, sleeping on friends' floors, the back of an old Kombi van and cheap hotels when it broke down, I heaved a sigh to once more be part of a family. Ben and his brothers had built this house for Tilly, a big house, with large rooms and two bathrooms. Grandma, with her thick, Scottish brogue (we shared the upstairs with her), four children, Ben and Tilly and this couple from the end of the earth. We began to laugh and relax. When I told her I was pregnant, Tilly immediately took me to the doctor who had delivered her own children.

He was a large, gentle man, but very firm when he thought that I was already four months pregnant and had been travelling for that time. I arrogantly assured him that I came from a line of sturdy Somerset and German farmers.

Tilly loved the *Ed Sullivan Show*, the music, the laughter and the dancing. She had taught herself to play the piano and had quick, nimble fingers. Organised and practical, she could cut, prepare and cook a meal with total efficiency for us all every night, just as she did her shopping, quickly and neatly.

The washing machine and dryer went non-stop, the kettle was always whistling, there was always a rush to get more milk for the kids and the cats and more bread for the freezer. (It was the first time I had seen packets of frozen bread dough for rolls.) A car was essential for shopping, one of those enormous family sitcom station wagons which swallowed Tilly when she got behind the wheel. But she drove competently and skilfully like she did everything else. I grew to love her dearly. She was the older sister I had never had and I shared everything with her.

We would sit at night in front of the large colour TV and I would watch fascinated as she knitted, fingers flashing, needles weaving in and out. She knitted sweaters for her family and her nieces and nephews and would curl into her favourite chair, neat fluffy slippers (always pink) covering the longest toes I had ever seen, a glass of brandy and dry or white wine on the table beside her. After the rendition of a sentimental song, she would look up from her knitting and whisper, 'Wasn't that just beautiful,' a wistful smile distracting her momentarily from knit one, purl one, pass the slip stitch over.

Tilly found many beautiful things about life. She had the willingness to think the best of people. I was more cynical and wary. I think of her now and there is an ache of missing. She and Ben knitted us into the fabric of their lives with acceptance and generosity.

Telegrams arrived from Washington DC inquiring how we would leave the country and advising us that we were required to remove our persons and chattels within twenty-four hours. In a panic, I phoned your office. Your big boss had contacts with the Democrats who were in power. So strings were pulled, phone calls made to Washington and eventually you were declared to be working on an essential federal contract. We applied for green cards. To get our status, we went through a senator in Washington, at that time a Democrat. He had signed our papers after Providence's assistant mayor and your engineering firm had gone as guarantors for our immigrant status.

Your set of fingerprints proved OK. Mine had not worked, so I had to go down to the local police station to have mine taken again. Mickey Spillane territory. I entered the Regency-looking building and saw desks scattered everywhere, serious men sitting behind them answering shrilling telephones that rang non-stop. 'Where, ma'am? Just give me the facts, ma'am.' They sat in trench coats and hats ready for action or in shirt sleeves as I walked in to ask directions.

'I've come for fingerprints,' I said quietly, but every eye seemed to look up and stare through me.

'This way, ma'am.' An overweight giant of a man opened a locked gate for me.

A room full of eyes followed my walk from the entrance to the door at the back of the room under the glare of fluorescent lights. I was being led back to the cells where the fingerprint equipment was kept. Past the cells, the drunks banging the bars, the stench of urine and stale clothes.

'Give us yer fingers. We know where to put 'em.'

'Share my bed, I'll make room. She don't look like no whore.'
I resisted the invitations.

'Shut up, you lot,' the officer leading the way advised.

All this to become a permanent alien. Thank God, the fingerprint area, a dirty table beside a dirty washbasin with a dirty towel. Purple fingers pressed and rolled hard as my hand is held by the calloused hand of a cop.

'That's it, girlie, I'll take you out the back way so's you don't have to listen to those foul creatures.'

Daylight at last but that was not the end of it. Once it was proved that I did have fingerprints, it was off to the courthouse, built in grand Georgian style with domes and columns and sculptures. Stand in front of the judge, put my hand across my heart and swear that I have not belonged to the Communist party or any other illegal organisation. Concentrate on the flag and promise to obey the American Constitution. Hand across my heart? I grinned, trying to figure out which side of my chest my heart was beating.

'So you think this is funny?' The black-frocked judge stared down at me.

'No, sir. I smile because I am honoured.'

Quick thinking, manipulate the words, fit them into the right context, fast. We became permanent aliens with green cards.

Now we return as foreigners with an American daughter. She has the passport, we have tourist visas and no longer desire to stay. Our lives have been made in Australia, but we will continue to return to America, to people and places which are a precious piece of our past

CHAPTER 12

It is very easy to fall into the pattern of life in Ben and Tilly's house, where we once again have been welcomed and loved. The language is a version of English and up north most of the accents are gentle and easy to understand. It is strange, though, to look at their children whom we knew as small children but who are now the same ages we were when we first came to America. So many years in between. To look at our friends and accept their age means that we must accept our own. I am frightened by this when I see the reflection of my face in the car window as we drive to the lake to satisfy the memories. Ben and Tilly are driving with us and are as excited as we are, I think they hope to recapture the joy and the fun we shared with them during the years we lived there.

Each time we return to America, we meet our old friend Tony. Tonight we will also meet his partner, Daisy, whom he has never mentioned before but with whom he has lived for twelve years. He has cancer. It is one of the reasons we have returned again to America, to see Tony as well as visiting Ben and Tilly (she has been very ill with a triple bypass heart operation.)

We met Tony before he had married his second wife. In fact, you were best man at his wedding to the exquisite, black-haired Nadine. Her glossy mane reached below her waist and she had black eyes and cream skin. All of her students fell in love with Nadine, their Russian teacher.

Tony, with the icy penetrating blue eyes, Rasputin beard and shy smile had fallen in love with her. They would visit us by the lake and Tony would sit holding her hand, looking at her adoringly, but she could not live with the eccentricities of the wild-looking Tony, although they are still good friends. He had been in Cuba as Castro came to power and he had been in the Argentine a year before Eva Peron died. He was the only capitalist communist American I ever met.

I met Tony and Nadine at a miserable time. I had lost the second baby and was so depressed I sometimes didn't want to get out of bed. I had felt life move inside me again and suddenly it was gone, stopped moving. There had to be something wrong with me. Everybody could have babies, it was easy. Had I done something to myself with those years of travelling? Was it my fault? In anger and panic one night, I got into the car and drove along dark country roads. I had no sense of direction or why I was going that way. I hadn't even left you a note. What could I have said? I had no words to describe how I was feeling.

My hands clutched the steering wheel and the engine hummed. I became totally lost. My sense of direction is non-existent, you know that. I saw a sign that made me realise that in my blind panic, I had driven into Connecticut. I had no idea how I had driven there.

Suddenly I became aware of the darkness. The trees were threatening, everything was closed, my whole body was shaking and I was sobbing.

I had driven anywhere just to get away, to escape, but there was no escape. It was part of me, inside my own malfunctioning body.

There was me, the car, and the dark and the road and I had no idea how to get back to the lake. I realised that you must be panicking. Pulling over, I turned off the ignition, locked the doors, turned on the radio and waited for the dawn. It was lucky that it was fall and not winter. I don't like being alone, I'm not very brave. I had to find my way back to the lake. I needed your comfort and love. I needed you to say, 'It's all right, we'll manage.' You are the university baseball blue's captain who bought me violets, who wanted me with single-minded passion and determination, who can't sing but who loves opera.

It is light. So much becomes clear in the very early light of day. I am stiff, cold and hungry. I start the car. You will be worrying. I must phone, get some coffee. I turn the Mustang around and drive looking for a gas station. How will you get to work?

Francine, a friend I had made in the first block of flats we moved into after leaving Ben and Tilly's house, had phoned you at the lake to chat and see how I was coping with the pregnancy. Instead, she had spent minutes calming your frantic worry. You told her that I had miscarried in hospital seven days ago, that I had gone out but not left a note. By dawn, you were panicking. Francine, Simon, their friends Tony and Nadine drove out to the cottage to see what had happened and were there when I phoned.

'I'm all right. Don't worry. I had to get away.'

'Where are you? We'll come and get you. Don't move.'

That is how we had met Tony and his beautiful lady. He decided that I needed a job to take my mind off things. He was a kind man who sat me behind the telephone, got me involved in talking to people, taking orders, being efficient for his Dine-out Club business which was a new venture in the National Bank building downtown. It was the early days and we worked in one cramped room. There was a staff of three and hundreds of cardboard boxes full of Dine-Out forms to be dispatched to businesses and associations.

Actually, he was probably shrewd. Businesses were prepared to listen to my sales pitch because of my different accent. But he was generous, such a generous man who never got angry and who paid me way above the hourly rate. He had the most open smile of any man I had ever met. Shy, yet knowing, his lips would widen and his eyes blaze an extra blue. His smile engaged his whole face. It was not a social smile, but a deep smile that made you feel he was giving you part of himself. He did not smile readily but I felt especially privileged when he smiled at you and me.

My father used to say, 'A smile costs nothing but pays great dividends.' In Tony's case, he was right.

You and Tony were the oddest pair of friends, he with his wild look and you with such a conservative upbringing and attitudes. In America in the sixties, however, anyone from Australia was immediately considered exotic.

'Yes,' you confirmed for him, 'there are definitely kangaroos in the main streets of Adelaide.'

I think he still wants to believe you.

'Come back and live here again,' he pleads, knowing that it is not possible to return to the past.

We often wondered if Tony was listed by the CIA because of his Cuban connection and his wanderings in the Argentine. He was in the south in the fifties, in Miami and New Orleans, renting squalid rooms because he had no money, bullied by cops who didn't like anyone from the north, let alone a young, poor male.

'Things haven't changed there,' he reckons. Now he informs us that he has sold his company and is going to establish an art gallery for charity. His business has extended from one room to an entire floor and there are offices in many States.

Tonight, I smile at Tony and his partner, Daisy, as we sit in an Italian restaurant in downtown Providence, where in 1636 Roger Williams declared it a haven for persecuted religious dissenters on the land of the Narragansett Indians. Tony has tamed, despite the long beard which is now grey and wiry. He is proud of the city and has shown us the cherry trees and the landscape planning along the river. They do not seem right together, he the dying eccentric millionaire, she the sweet, attractive worker for Blue Cross Medical System. She has three children, one son a tattoo artist who advertises on the internet, a son who works in children's toys after studying engineering, and a beautiful daughter, a lifeguard who is learning to drive and getting straight As at school. Her elder son will tattoo dragons, mystic figures, swords (hygienically, of course) and she shows me the rose on her ankle.

It is strange to see Tony, sitting so benevolent, generous in the middle of family talk with his wild beard and white hair and memories of Eva Peron when he was twenty-two, when he was sweating in a stifling room and the Louisiana cops were dangerous, poorly paid and violent towards outsiders, especially damn Yankees.

We eat Thai noodles and polenta and Italian sausage, Tony eats beans and salad. His strict non-fat diet is supposed to control the cancer that is running riot in his body. He talks proudly of the massive redevelopment of downtown, one of the oldest cities in the USA. When the colonies began to break with England, Providence became a leader of the resistance movement. In 1775, rebels burned tea in Market Square where we walked tonight to get to the restaurant. It is strange to think that Providence began as an Anglo-Saxon Protestant environment – the Celtic element, the Irish Catholic influence is now so strong. Apart from the Yankees, Germans, French Canadians, Swedes, Portuguese and Italians, British as well as the Irish make up Rhode Island's population. They were attracted in the forties by the manufacture of jewellery and production of woollen and worsted goods.

Splendid mansions were built along tree-lined Elmwood Avenue, Blackstone Boulevard, Westminster Street and Broadway. Providence enjoyed wealthy entrepreneurs and investors. But there is a curious lack of energy, almost a deserted feeling in the place as we walk back to Tony's garage where the cars are parked. The mall is no longer where I went to work every day at Elizabeth Jones Career and Fashion School after I decided to leave the Dine-out business and do something different. Tony had seemed pleased that I was excited by a new challenge, and had encouraged me to apply for the job.

The school is no longer. Despite the water gardens and fountains along the river that used to be foul and sluggish and the soaring Westin Hotel like a wedding cake sparkling level upon level and the flowering cherry trees along the towpath, much is now run-down, stores are closed or selling trash. Yet I still hear the laughter as we beautiful girls from the modelling school flaunted our way around town.

CHAPTER 13

We had spent 1967 Thanksgiving with Tilly and Ben. I sat with morning coffee out on the porch reading the *Providence Journal* and I saw an advertisement for a receptionist in a fashion school. I applied, basing my application on one week's reception work in a railway station in London and Tony's reference.

The north-east coast of America is a conservative place. Tony hadn't minded what I wore to work. In fact, he encouraged my different look. I had worked in London, swinging in the sixties, where mini-skirts were the rage. I had not expected the below the knee skirts, the matronly dresses with every man downtown wearing a suit. I had associated the north-east coast with New York and the avant-garde. I had forgotten that Boston was the home of the Pilgrim Fathers and I was to learn that Rhode Island was very Irish Catholic. I dressed in London gear, a leather mini and black stockings, put on my most refined accent and caught the bus to the interview. I was to learn that public prudishness had nothing to do with the double standards of corrupt business practices.

Joe Bufolino was swarthy, triple-chinned with a pugnacious face and small blue eyes. He was wearing an Italian suit and white shirt with a gaudy wide tie, double-knotted. His hands were smooth and manicured. I noticed them as he sat ponderously behind the desk tapping his fingers together. They were long, unlike the rest of the man. He sat swivelling authoritatively.

'You can take shorthand?'

'Yes, Australian shorthand,' I lied.

'You can type?'

'Yes,' I had done a two-week night course in Australia.

'You can use a switchboard?'

'Yes, an English switchboard,' I lied.

'Walk.'

I did as I was commanded, walked self-consciously up and down in front of him.

'You got great legs but you walk like your pants are full of shit. You got the job. Lose your accent and you're finished.'

'Yes sir, no sir.'

Mr Joe Bufolino became my boss. He would send me out to buy things I had never heard of just to hear me say them and laugh at my confusion when I didn't know where to buy them.

'Lily, buy me a submarine.' Really?

'Elizabeth Jones Career and Fashion School, may I help you please?' My regular spiel as I desperately attempted to cope with shorthand and typing and a switchboard that never seemed to stop ringing.

'Oh, jeez no, lady, just keep talkin', I wanna hear ya talkin'.'

That made things easier. I did plenty of talking. I had to learn to sell myself and the school, feeling funny about it the whole time. But this was America, I learned fast to sell the idea of myself. I learned to pitch myself to the customer. After all, we were living within commuting distance of the Boston Redsox and I was married to a man who loved and played baseball. The pitcher is the focus of the baseball game and if he doesn't pitch well, the team loses.

Pitch. It's a strange word, meaning anything from a black, tenacious resinous substance, to erecting a tent, to a vigorous argument, to falling heavily on one's head, to a mode of delivery, to 'little pitchers have long ears' when things not to be heard are overheard by children. The Oxford dictionary does not talk about pitching an idea or oneself. It must be an American idiom. I learned to listen to people who presented their ideas and themselves as if they were the best, most innovative, most desirable in the world. I learned quickly to understand the national pride of being an American; that to most Americans, America is the world.

The first floor was the reception and interview area. The next floor was the photography, lecture rooms and shoots for the models with wardrobes and props. We were told we had to put portfolios together, and when the boss realised I was university educated and qualified in speech arts to teach the models, he decided, 'Hey, Lily, you can teach them to speak right. Forget this stuff.'

They hired another receptionist and I prepared lectures at home by the lake to be submitted to the company directors. Suddenly, I had become a person with status and my boss was not sure any longer how to treat me. I had been to university and he no longer asked me to fetch pastrami on rye or go to the twenty-four-hour bar next door to get his cigarettes. I would have to pass tables where men were already bleary eyed at eleven o'clock in the morning. They stared at me, their eyes stripping me naked as I stumbled in the dark towards the bar to buy Cuban cigarillos. I stayed aloof and did not smile.

I taught girls of mostly Italian or Portuguese descent, many of them overweight and shy. Elizabeth Jones Career and Fashion School was a finishing school before they found husbands.

Georgio was my friend up on the photography floor. Nuggetty, white skinned and black-eyed, Georgio had that rolling mellow accent of the American Italian. 'Lily, I can get ya anythink ya want. Teevee, radio, frigerator, you name it, I can get it. We got storehouses of stuff in Pawtucket.' Owning things is next to godliness in America, but it's no big deal. Things are for using and making life comfortable and they're cheap. I got lost in Ann and Hope. It was the hugest discount store I had ever seen and the car park on site was colossal and terrifying, acres of cars parked side by side and end to end.

The big boss from Chicago, came to look over the school. He was a small, round man with a trimmed moustache and small feet. His hair was black, parted on the side, and it flopped across his forehead. With an almost girlish toss, he would flip it out of his eyes. He smiled often, especially when he was issuing instructions. 'Hey, Lily, cum hereya.' His body, held together in a classical Italian suit, pushed me against the window. 'Look through the window. See my Cadillac. Do I need more money in the meter? Here, take these dimes and feed it, will ya?' His soft body pressed into me forcing me onto the window ledge and against the glass.

'Hey, my boat's at Newport, I got a place there, come down on the weekend. We'll have a good time.' The order had been given. He wanted more than a walk on the cliff.

Embarrassed and angry, I told him I'd have to think about it. I couldn't tell him I was pregnant. I had a feeling the time was coming when I would need to say goodbye to Elizabeth Jones Career and Fashion School.

I had heard rumours about Mafia money and Georgio had said, 'Lily, don't let them take your photo. You don't know where you'll end up, your head on someone else's body, screwing someone you've never seen. Dirty pictures are big money.'

CHAPTER 14

Money seemed to rule everything and everybody in America in the sixties despite the flower power revolution. It fascinated me watching the way people spent money. There had been no giant supermarkets in Australia when I had left, so the supermarkets and giant discount stores like Apex and Ann and Hope were overwhelming. I watched people, pushed into shorts and T-shirts, with bulging breasts and bottoms, struggle with wire trolleys piled high with cigarette cartons, buckets, towels, lingerie, cutlery, deep-frozen vegetables, suits, umbrellas, frozen bread mix, sneakers, tracksuits, bedside lamps, electric frypans, beds and dresses. You name it, you could buy it if you had the money. Usually everything was piled into the back of a station wagon, driven by a woman, with the man in the passenger seat. I knew women in Australia who were too afraid to drive and couldn't afford a car even if they could drive.

The stores were open all day Saturday and Sunday. We could spend money any time we felt like shopping. Men in T-shirts, jeans and lumber jackets and sneakers, women with their hair in curlers and chewing gum that was the fashion of the discount store. If you had real money, you had power. If you didn't have it, you were nobody. The Kennedys were the epitome of money and power. I was told the rumour that old man Kennedy had been a rum runner on the coast of Rhode Island, that that is what started the Kennedy money. I heard rumours of slave trading along the same coast. The Kennedy compound at Martha's Vineyard was sealed off from the outside world. Money created their power and exclusivity. (Money and power hadn't stopped John Kennedy in 1962, and later in June 1968, his brother Robert, from being assassinated.)

Some of the hippies in San Francisco's Height Ashbury were very wealthy people. It was a lifestyle that attracted film stars and entertainers and their wealthy offspring as well as the children of middle-class America. They didn't call it flower power for nothing. They had the money to preach love and peace and paint quaint weatherboard houses gaudy colours and get stoned to the sounds of Jimi Hendrix, Jefferson Airplane, Joan Baez, Crosby, Stills, Nash and Young, Canned Heat… Peace, man, and love.

I read in August 1969 that a Woodstock Musical Festival was to be held in a farmer's field near Bethel in the Catskill Mountains in upstate New York. Half a million people attended. There was no violence, no thieving. Thousands smoked pot and dropped acid. Friends Lucy and David had said, 'Come with us.'

We didn't go, it was hardly the place to take a baby, but we are able to say, 'I didn't go to Woodstock but my friends David and Lucy went.' That's almost the same thing.

I bought the first LP records that came out of Woodstock and felt exhilarated, playing the tracks over and over. 'Marrakesh Express', 'Let the Sunshine In', 'My Beautiful People', the 'Birthday of the Sun'. The Beatles, Mia Farrow, the Rolling Stones all committed to the teachings of the Maharishi Mahesh Yogi. Transcendental meditation became the big turn-on for the wealthy in Hollywood and for the young.

We were young. What we didn't understand then was that we were part of a revolt against the rules with the comfort of full employment and material affluence. We could challenge everything because materially, we were not risking much. The ones who were risking everything were the people who being sent to fight in Vietnam. They were the ones caught tight within the system of rules, the corruptions and the conspiracies.

When President Johnson ordered no more bombing raids over North Vietnam in April 1968, stoned students who had dropped out chanted, 'Hey, hey, LBJ, how many kids have you killed today? Peace.' It was the Age of Aquarius while eighteen-year-olds were being sprayed with Agent Orange in Vietnam. Anger was simmering in America. We lived by the lake in a cocoon.

The chances were there to make money or be a success if you had the ideas and the drive. People never said, as they did in Australia, 'Do you think that's a good idea?' and then continue to squash it with problems they foresee. When I developed the communication skills course in America for Elizabeth Jones Career and Fashion School, it was received with enthusiasm and several sources put money into its development and packaging. When I returned to Australia in the late seventies and was interviewed on Melbourne television, the concept was ridiculed. 'So you want to teach women to talk? Ha, ha, ha.'

I felt angry and humiliated and wondered what sort of country I had returned to, until women began to stop me on St Kilda Beach and in the shopping centres asking for help, while the YMCA decided to promote courses which I ran. Australia feels uncomfortable with its tall poppies. America is a country which loves its Tall Poppies and nourishes them and their ideas. They also assassinate them.

Riding home on the bus one day after my talk with George, I was wondering about my future with the Elizabeth Jones Career and Fashion School. It had been a fantastic experience but the ice was cracking and I was starting to see the murk underneath. I was frightened. There had also been several demonstrations by Blacks in downtown and you did not want me travelling at night. You said that it wasn't safe.

I usually sat next to an Iroquois Indian, named Matti, who was a construction worker. He and his brother worked on tall building sites in downtown. He said the Iroquois have no fear of heights. 'My brother has fallen, I go to visit him often'. That is why I saw him on the bus every day, going to the hospital.

'Don't get mixed up with the Mafia, they're bad, I know people who got to pay them protection to be able to build anything,' he warned.

I was one of the few white women who caught the bus. The others were mostly Blacks and a few Indians. It was a strange feeling coming from a culture so predominantly white. I'd never sat next to a black person before. I stuck out like the proverbial thumb, dressed to go to work in a fashion school as well as being white.

Everyone at work thought that I was eccentric. They never caught buses, would never be caught dead riding in one.

It was the year before Neil Armstrong walked on the moon, but to many Americans the country was going haywire. I watched it all on television, the first time we had owned a set, a colour TV. After the death of Martin Luther King, killed by James Earl Ray in Memphis, I saw cities smouldering, angry Blacks looting and smashing. There were ugly scenes in downtown Providence.

I was abused one evening by a man who had stopped his Cadillac suddenly in Canal Street and I had touched his back fender. He pulled his car to a screeching halt, left it in the middle of the road and strode over to me. I got out of the car, ready to show him my licence and insurance papers and to say that I was sorry. His face turned red and he screamed at me that I had deliberately hit him because he had a Cadillac and had New York number plates.

When he heard my accent, he yelled, 'Get home. You ain't got no right in this country!'

A crowd had gathered and when he called me a 'pinko' they started to shout and hiss and shake their fists at him when I started to cry.

I can still see his face, pushing up at mine so close I could see the sweat in the creases around his mouth and his bad teeth and the hairs up his broad nose. Black hairs in wide nostrils, gut hanging over his narrow, leather belt, black, thick hair on the back of his hands. I walked over to his car to inspect the damage, a crowd behind me. No one could find a mark.

His simmering anger reminded me of the border guard. I was a convenient target. I began to feel angry, but vulnerable, very, very alone, and he had my name and address. But I never heard another thing. He didn't own the car, he was a chauffeur. Your big boss was a friend of the owner of the car.

'He won't speak to any woman like that again,' he promised you. I wondered what I had started but never inquired any further.

You said, 'Give it up. We don't need the money. Look what

happened to Emily and Howie,' our friends who had gone into the restaurant business. We had given them Uncle Rocco's warning, but they hadn't listened.

You used to park the car up on Federal Hill when you were working downtown. You came home to the lake shaking one night. Walking back to the car, you had stumbled into a police guard protecting witnesses at the Barbosa trials of the New England mafia being held in Providence. Police lined either side of the courthouse holding submachine guns at the ready. There was no one else, only you walking down the road with your briefcase and car keys. You said that you started to sweat and shake and walked down the middle of the road holding your briefcase and with your other arm stiff by your side. You said you were afraid that if you sneezed or put a hand in your pocket, the police would shoot. You couldn't wait to get home to the lake.

CHAPTER 15

When we had signed the papers to rent the house by the lake, Ben and Tilly came to help us clean it up. The doctor had left it in a mess. They had polished and scrubbed and helped us unpack our boxes and few possessions.

'You have found a magic place. We didn't know anything like this existed in Rhode Island.'

Ben and Tilly had not liked our apartment in Garden City. They felt that it was full of nouveau riche ex-New Yorkers and wealthy Italian Americans. Ben was from an old New England family and despite her soft American drawl there was still the touch of Scottish brogue when Tilly spoke. Together, we discovered the names carved into the back door of the linen cupboard, all the names of people who had lived in the cottage. We immediately carved our names.

We felt safe by the lake. It was our private world, where we invited only the people we liked and trusted. You did teach me how to shoot a gun, but I shot a hole in the wardrobe. You nearly did worse than that! It was a wonderful New England night. No wind, so calm on the lake. We had sat down on the deck with Emma feeding the ducks and we had sailed in the boat up and down the lake. We weren't going to the Newport yacht races. We had our water and our boat at our back doorstep.

Often we swam naked when the water was warm and made love on the deck under the stars. Our bodies were so young and firm we couldn't get enough of each other and at night we would fall asleep in bed satiated and entangled together. It was early morning, everything was quiet except for our deep breathing. There was a loud thud.

'It's someone breaking in,' I hissed in your ear, suddenly awake.

We were both shaking because we could hear someone still pushing at a downstairs window. Perhaps they thought the house was unoccupied, or a soft target being so isolated. You rolled out of bed naked, grabbed a pair of jeans and, as you pulled them on, I reached into the wardrobe to pull the gun out from under the ski gear where I had hidden it.

In the dark, you ran downstairs barefoot, holding a loaded gun. A leg was through the window. The wire screen was off and it had been forced open.

'Don't move, or I will shoot!' You sounded so angry. You pushed the gun against the body of the intruder.

'For Christ sake, it's me. Don't shoot! It's Hugh! Your brother! Don't shoot!'

'What the hell do you think you're doing? Where have you come from? Why didn't you knock on the door like a normal person? I was going to shoot!' You clicked the safety latch on the gun and dropped it on the sofa under the window. 'Get your leg out. Go to the door. Why didn't you knock? God damn you, you know we've got a baby here. What stupid game are you playing? We haven't heard from you for months.'

'I've driven up from Newport, didn't want to disturb you. Knew you'd be asleep. Thought I'd creep in and sleep on the sofa but you'd locked the door.'

He was either stoned or drunk, but I remember that I was terrified at how easily our feeling of security had been destroyed.

He'd gone to the Newport yacht races and thought it would be easier to crash with us after a hard few days of drinking and socialising. I remember that night as if it was yesterday. It had been easy to buy a hand gun at one of the big discount stores. I wrapped it up in a blanket and hid it away but I could always see it lying there in my mind. You eventually sold it at a garage sale.

CHAPTER 16

Eleanor and Connor were people we trusted. We had met them through Uncle Rocco and Lisa Jean and they had become good friends.

She was an Australian war bride who had been having an affair with the very Catholic Connor for twenty years. Connor was a big undertaker in Rhode Island, a large, Irish American who was cheerful and very generous. He offered to be sponsor for our green cards, which were more precious than the emeralds Lori traded in her jewellery business.

Connor had been in the funeral business since he was eleven. He started delivering flowers to wakes, had risen to embalmer and now owned the business behind the building with the enormous Gothic facade of columns and carved wooden doors up in North Providence. He loved Lori, a gentle, red-haired and quietly spoken woman, and because of that he agreed to be our sponsor.

I took the immigration forms to Connor, driving our newly bought nearly new gold Mustang with the black top. 'Keep to the right, keep to the right.' I warned myself as I purred along with the automatic left hand drive, feeling like a million dollars.

I waited in the reception. 'What a grand building,' I wondered, 'for people who are already dead.' Then realised that it was really a building for the living who love or fear the dead.

There was a small jar on a shelf which fascinated me. I was looking at it when Connor came out of his office to meet me, dressed in a sombre three- piece suit.

'Hello, my dear. It's so good to see you!' His hug was warm and friendly. He was a tall man who obviously loved his food. He smelled of delicious, expensive aftershave lotion.

'Connor, thank you so much for what you're prepared to do for us. We really appreciate it.'

'You're friends of Eleanor's, that's enough for me.'

'What is that jar, Connor?'

'That's a jar of ashes that has never been claimed. It's stood there since 1952. No one's claimed them. They're the ashes of an eleven-year old boy, same age as me when I started to work here. I keep them here to remind myself of the ultimate end and my beginning. I enjoy life.

Come. I'll show you around. Have you got the papers?' He signed them, no questions asked.

I had dressed carefully to visit this important person. A very important person to us. I had already straightened my curly mop with Max Factor hair straightener used by the black women and it hung long over my shoulders now that it was straight. Grey, I had thought, yes, grey would be appropriate. So I had dressed in a wide-legged grey jump suit with a long-sleeved, white Elizabethan blouse and black boots. I wore beads like the hippies we had seen wandering in New York's East Village where, beaded, sandalled, smoking dope, they wandered around in loose-fitting clothes calling out 'Peace, man.' But my outfit was nothing like their outfits or the wardrobe I was about to see, although my black eye make-up and pale lipstick was probably corpse-like. I was glad that I hadn't worn flowers in my hair.

'Would you like me to show you around?' I was proudly offered and could hardly say no.

So the tour of the undertaking business began. Through the wardrobe room with the racks of pale blue and pink and oyster-coloured satin gowns and rows of wigs, the make-up room, the coffin sales room, all huge and quiet, to the embalming room.

The embalmer was small, bent, wizened and cross-eyed (he looked like an embalmed body himself) and was stitching up a wealthy Italian male who had died of cancer to make him look deadly alive, not a pretty sight. In Catholic Rhode Island, the wake is an important part of the burial.

The director of your company died and was prepared for the wake by Connor. You went to the wake, the first one you had ever attended.

Your boss's son had died not long before speeding down the freeway to Cape Cod the wrong side of the road at night. They said it was LSD. He had had a bad trip on lysergic acid diethylamide, the hallucinogenic drug of the sixties promoted by Dr Timothy Leary, turning on stars like John Lennon. It seemed sad to me that the slogans 'flower power' and 'make love not war' became inextricably mixed with the drug culture.

The hippies and the love generation in Haight and Ashbury Streets and New York's East Village seemed incapable of separating peace and love from being stoned.

'Don't die in winter,' Connor warned. 'It costs twice as much to be buried because they have to bring in the jackhammers to get through the frozen ground.'

Lori's daughter and granddaughter were burned in a fire in winter. Their weatherboard apartment caught alight in winter with faulty heating and they never had a chance. She gave me rings. Every time I wear them, I think of her and the great sadness behind her smile.

'Lily, would you let Connor and me use your house by the lake for the weekend? We need to have a party and he's married and it's very hard. Your house is so hidden away. We'll put you up in the downtown Biltmore.' It was the first time Lori had ever asked anything from us.

I was just pregnant with my second child and everything was going well. We never had the money to stay anywhere grand like the downtown hotel. It had been years of sleeping in an attic flat in London or travelling in an ancient Kombi van and sleeping in the back of it. When it broke down, we would look for the cheapest accommodation wherever we happened to be. We had been part of that European tribe of young people in the sixties who wandered and explored with two bob in their pockets and only a vague idea of where they might end up. A weekend in the Biltmore, with its exotic history, would be a welcome luxury.

We knew the Providence Biltmore in Kennedy Plaza was an historic landmark known as the 'Grand Dame of Providence'. An art deco building, opened in 1922, it was the place to stay in the sixties although run-down from its former glory. Business people and Brown University parents and alumni stayed there when they came to Providence. In the sixties, the Biltmore was only a shadow of the magnificent hotel it had been in the twenties. You had eaten, once, with your boss in the Falstaff Room, a restaurant in the hotel, primarily frequented by men, and although the Bacchante Room was still in operation, the era of the Bacchante Girls had finished. Your boss said that they had been famous, known for their beauty and their poise (and legs!).

The Bacchante Room had dimmed lights and mirrored walls. Seating sections were called 'banquettes' and when a button was pushed, a Bacchante girl would appear in costume, featuring diaphanous, see through skirts. The bar had a glass floor which was underlit with pink lighting, showing off the girls' legs.

'Just my luck, born in the wrong age,' you grinned at the photos in the foyer.

We would be eating in the Canary Room, which served a more upscale clientele. The Town Room was a medium-priced dining place open to the public, but this was to be our special weekend. We were going upmarket in every way. After all, we would be sleeping in the same hotel where John Kennedy and President Lyndon Johnson had snored and shaved.

The Biltmore was still a landmark in Providence, within walking distance of the State Capitol, the Rhode Island School of Design, Brown University and Federal Hill, where the Justice Department and State Legislature buildings are prominent. In the sixties, it was the place to be seen, chatting in the three-storeyed lobby with its grand staircase or riding in the elevator down to the desk below curved, gilded ceilings, massive chandeliers and mahogany balconies. It was as close to a palace as you could get in Providence. We were going to gorge ourselves on the lavish Sunday brunch and have champagne cocktails. I would wear the same black dress for each occasion and hope that nobody noticed.

I felt worried that I just wouldn't look good enough in the middle of this sophisticated place.

'Just be yourself,' you said, 'just enjoy yourself. You're as good as any of them.'

The luxury of the king-size beds and enormous sheets and the endless stream of hot water and bubble bath made me feel that I never wanted to make a bed again. Heaven would surely be like this, with a king-size bed, clean sheets and huge, white fluffy towels every day and the bed made by someone else and the washing done by someone else and the cleaning done by someone else. Heaven! It made up for the tension I had felt in the grand foyer with costumed doormen and the efficient, smooth women behind the reception desk. Their long red fingernails warned efficiency and the practised smiles were a plastic welcome.

'Of course.' I was glad that we had said yes to Lori and Connor. What else could we have said to such generous people?

When we had first met Connor, he had taken us in his Cadillac to tour up the coast of New England and he had hired a launch to take us out onto Narragansett Sound. We left from the marina in Newport and sailed through Nantucket Sound, past Woods Hole and Hyannis up the curling tail of Cape Cod to Provincetown. He pointed out Chappaquiddick Island and Martha's Vineyard, and laughed about the Kennedy pretensions to greatness.

Lori and Connor could use the cottage whenever and for as long as they liked. I was learning not to judge, to let other people's experiences wash over me, to listen and to learn. There is no one way of living or looking at life; it is like living in a house of mirrors.

The leaves from the ash trees in fall made a thick, crunchy blanket around the cottage. We rolled in them, we made bonfires, we raked neat piles all over the place and jumped in them. They were brown and curled on the edges and we knew before long the soil would be frozen again and slippery and white.

Connor and Lori left the house full of food. Not any old food, but lobster meat and pâté, French cheeses and imported strawberries. The house was the cleanest it had ever been.

We had just revelled in luxury. Breakfast in bed would never be the same after fresh-squeezed orange juice and a basket of fresh-cooked pastries delivered by a liveried room service waiter. Sachets of hair shampoo and conditioner, tiny soaps in individual boxes, shower cap with the Biltmore stamp like the toothbrush and toothpaste container. White, lush towels to wrap right around a body that smelled enticing after a bath full of Biltmore perfumed bubbles.

I didn't want to leave. This was definitely the lifestyle meant for me. It is so good to know that the Providence Biltmore had been restored now to its 1920s elegance. The older I become, the more I appreciate the comforts of thick towels, good mattresses, food which someone else prepares beautifully and service. Water in our house by the lake came from a well and you were always worried about the pressure and that we might use up the supply, so splashing around in deep fragrant baths, was a supreme indulgence. You at one end, me at the other (I always got the end with the plug), scrubbing each other's backs.

Connor and Lori asked us to dinner at the Rhode Island Yacht Club one night after they had stayed at the lake. A place where only members and their friends could entertain. The kind of place that you and I would never enter unless invited, it represented a world that we knew nothing about. We skirted around the edges of the lifestyles of friends like Sam and Connor and Uncle Rocco and, later, my bosses at the fashion school.

Lori had a reason for inviting us. 'Lily, have you ever thought of working in a place like this?'

It was a cocoon, this club, like the lake was for us. It was a refuge for the white wealthy. I was pretty sure no Blacks and no Jewish people would be members. It was the sort of place people met to make deals, to exchange gossip, to make and ruin reputations of the powerful or would be powerful. It was a place of power and secrets.

'There's a position here you could buy.'

It was the first time I had heard of buying a job. I knew that in Europe and New York waiters bought positions in prestigious restaurants because the tips were so enormous.

'Buy?'

'You can make more money here than you ever dreamed of. They need a hat check girl, but you'll need to put money up front. I can put your name forward to the committee.'

These amazing people, these Americans, I love how they grab at life and give its throat a good rattle! Lori would not understand my hesitance. I looked at you.

'Con, Lori, is it all night work?'

'Yes, mostly.'

I was thinking of Lily, the hat check chick. My mind boggled, I had done some crazy jobs, but this would surely top them.

'Would I need to wear an outfit like a Playboy Club type thing?' I was going cold on the idea.

Every entertainment venue needed a hat check for coats and scarves and overshoes because of the cold and the snow in winter. All venues were so overbearingly heated that I felt like stripping as soon as I entered a door; one would roast in an overcoat. We had to learn to dress in layers, rarely wearing thick, woolly sweaters or jackets inside.

My greed was saying, 'Go for it!' My provincialism and caution was saying, 'Wait on, do I want the lifestyle that this will involve? Late nights, weekend work, what will that do to my marriage?' Deep down, I was scared of the lifestyle that I would become part of. The people who frequented the club, I only knew on the surface of their lives. But there would be an element of danger that would be fascinating. The promise of big tips was alluring, but surely they wouldn't be given just for checking in a man's coat and overshoes? More would be demanded than a cheerful Australian 'G'day.'

'They'd like you.' Connor was embarrassed. 'You'd need another car, though, at night. Don't know whether you like driving in winter.' He was looking at you hopefully, knights together, protecting their women.

'Nup, crazy idea,' you butted in.

I was angry that you would dare speak for me, but pleased that Connor had given a face-saving way out.

'I hate driving in the snow, at night.' I was mainly not happy about the idea of dressing up as a bimbo, that's not my style, plus I would probably belt the first customer who made a pass at me.

'Lori, you're wonderful for thinking of me, you are kind and generous. I'm going to say no. I'll look for a daytime job, perhaps I might even go back to university and do a Masters of English Literature. I've received an assessment of my Australian qualifications from Washington,'

'Good for you,' encouraged Connor.

You looked amazed, as I had not suggested any of these ideas yet to you. We were keeping news of the pregnancy quiet until we were certain that it would be all right.

Our conversation had been taking place in the usual haze of smoke. Everyone smoked. Connor and Lori smoked, I smoked. Long, filtertipped Alpine Menthol cigarettes. I thought that I was enjoying cheap sophistication at thirty-two cents a packet of twenty. Everyone smoked like the Hollywood film stars. no one thought anything of entering a room full of smoke haze. The first time I saw men smoking cigars was in America, particularly the owner of Elizabeth Jones Career and Fashion School. You never smoked – oh, occasionally you puffed on a pipe in front of the fire – but neither of us were hooked on tobacco and both gave it up painlessly years later.

We drove home, comfortable with my decision not to go for the job at the club, but I tickled with the thought, 'What if, what sort of exciting things might have happened to me in a job like that? Am I just being pathetic tying myself to a man?'

Lori and Connor made us aware of the layers to the lives of people we were meeting. There is an element of danger being in a strange place, not knowing the codes that bind particular people to one another. One has to use intuition and social cunning to know how to respond. To risk the smile and the handshake and the look in the eyes which might result in a relationship. I find that exciting, the risk taking, judging how much of self to reveal and share, never really sure of what might happen because the codes of social behaviour are different in every place with every person.

The social honesty of the Australians in London fascinated people there, while it was assumed by many that openness meant lack of social graces. The north-east coast of America had its own specific social codes and it was necessary to stand apart for a time to find one's place (in fact to decide if one wanted to find a place). I never stopped to ask myself what people might be thinking about me. I was busy learning about them.

CHAPTER 17

To create a social network, it was necessary to put out my roots sideways. So many of us in the sixties were rootless creatures, moving, exploring, moving again, sometimes dying in the exploration. I looked sideways to make connections. To put roots down in one place made it hard to pull up and move on (that is what I believed before I had a child). I thought that a shallow-rooted plant would flower as beautifully as a flower planted deeply which would take longer to blossom. In fact, often it won't blossom because the roots are too deep. I wanted to do as much, see as much, meet as many people as was possible in as many different places. After spending my youth in an Adelaide suburb, I had been hungry for foreign experiences. I had become the OS junkie and didn't realise it.

Our friends were a hugely diverse group of people. They wove in and out of our lives creating a magic carpet on which we rode. At the Biltmore, we had dined in the Canary room with Francine, my black haired friend: a Bunny Girl with enormous breasts and tiny waist who worked at Hugh Hefner's Providence Playboy Club. Frannie had the voice and giggle of a child, but the body of a siren. Men found her irresistible and she made the most of it. She eventually disappeared like so many people I knew in the late sixties and early seventies drug scene when she moved with Simon, her Jewish husband, to California. Moni is now white-haired and sells two-dollar bills to tourists (there is no such thing in American currency, but people fall for it all the time). He lives in a van and travels. The last time I heard from Fran, years ago, she was 'turning on' in the caves down in the Baja of southern California. But that night we dined on seafood cocktails and New York sirloins with jacket potatoes and Caesar salad and flaming crêpes cooked by the head waiter (a friend of Fran's) at the table.

Fran was fun. Fran and I and Rita Mae, we laughed so much together when we met in that apartment block in Garden City, Rhode Island, above Meshanticut Valley Parkway. The green trees had enticed us to the apartments, landscaped and fussed over, but still with a wild, forestry look. The apartments were built on a hillside and looked down over a shopping complex. (They were the early days before I had found the house by the lake and when we moved from Ben and Tilly's house in Massachusetts. We had lived on their hospitality for long enough.) We lived on a ground-floor apartment and the two-storeyed complex was in a U shape, painted white and surrounded with trees and grass. We thought it was beautiful.

I nearly set fire to the apartment and I met Fran and Rita Mae when they came to my rescue. We owned a mattress, a door on bricks for a coffee table and painted cardboard boxes for bedside tables. I didn't know what broil meant and I set fire to the meat, filling the place with smoke that set off the smoke alarms. She and Mae came rushing in and by the time the fire engines arrived, they had the fire out and me sitting at the kitchen table. One burly fireman would have filled the kitchen, but there were six of them and I felt a fool. They were generous in their understanding and one of them made a date with Franny.

She explained in her giggling, confidential way, 'She's foreign,' and they were satisfied.

Residents by this time were hanging over balconies because they had heard the sirens, but it was Franny and Mae who came to help. When they came to visit me by the lake, we sat on the porch and laughed about it. Fran took me swimming in the summer of '68 to the beach where they filmed *Jaws*. The hungry males parading past looked far more dangerous than the mechanical shark. How rude they were to Mae, who was tall, black and from Alabama.

She used to laugh at Francine and me as we sun baked on the lawn.

'You want to be my colour and I want to be yours,' she cackled. But there was little laughter in her life as a companion to the wealthy and elderly Mrs Grimaldi. I was abused for treating her as a friend. She brought me swamp moss back from Alabama when she went to visit her family and cried when Martin Luther King and Robert Kennedy were shot. We drove her to church for a service for Robert Kennedy because none of the Christians in her church were prepared to take her. Martin Luther King had been shot in Memphis in April 1968 and James Earl Ray had been arrested for his murder and sentenced to ninety-nine years gaol.

We moved to the lake as hundreds of riots were taking place and the army had been called out to keep order in Washington, Baltimore and Chicago. No Blacks lived anywhere near the lake, that was WASP Country.

The first time I had used the laundromat at the apartment complex, when we had just moved in, an elderly resident had approached me.

'You know we got a nigger here?'

'You mean my friend, Rita Mae?'

'You know they're supposed to do it better than white women.'

To control my rage, I had concentrated on the clothes churning round and round like my twisting stomach. I had muttered, 'I wouldn't know.' I hated these ugly people.

Mae taught me how to wash the large picture windows without leaving streaks and I made her a collage of the first moon landing. She would sit with me on our stoop and talk about her life while I painted large black abstracts to cover our white, bare walls in the apartment. I successfully covered our minuscule kitchen wall without having to do a painting when I bought a squid and tried to clean it. I had no idea what I was doing and sprayed squid ink everywhere. My neighbours on either side burst out laughing, but helped me to repaint the walls before rent day.

There was so much I didn't know, just because we spoke English. The meanings were different for so many things in my world. I reciprocated friendliness with friendliness, but was warned by your boss that I was too smiley, that's why the second-hand car dealer thought that I would be on for an afternoon in the motel where he and his fellow sleazes took their bits on the side. He'd sold us the Mustang but obviously thought that he was due extra commission.

It was Spring when we bought the Mustang before we had moved to Rhode Island from Massachusetts. We were embarrassed depending on Ben and Tilly Hayston for transport, so decided to look for a car to buy, to help us look for an apartment. It lured us, standing shiny on display in the car yard, a Dealer's Special. That's what we were told by Jo Wenzel. Before we knew it, we had signed papers and were its owners without having so much as taken it for a test drive or possessing American driving licences.

A slimy toad, Jo Wenzel had bitten fingernails, heavy gold rings and when he groped at my body it made me shudder. He had insisted on calling in to make sure that we were managing the car OK. After all, we were foreign and had never driven in America before. He was just being helpful and friendly and wouldn't I like to go to the motel with him. You told him to keep away. I avoided driving past the car yard just in case he might be anywhere around. But I loved driving the Mustang, changing the stick shift as I changed lanes on the freeway.

It was the most sexy car we had ever owned, after uncle Sid's buckboard, the orange Mini and the old Kombi van. (You had sold it to a crummy car dealer in Putney for one hundred and twenty pounds the day before we flew out from England to Canada. The Inland Revenue hunted you for years). The Mustang was sleek and exciting. Ben and Tilly thought we were mad. They didn't understand that the gold, black hooded mean machine with the floor stick shift made us feel that we had really arrived in America. The second time I drove, still on my international driver's licence, I had to drive on the freeway when I went to pick up our trunks that had come from England by sea. I couldn't see out the back or the sides and drove in the middle lane offering prayers whenever I had to change lanes or make an exit. Somehow, the car, the trunks and I made it safely back to the apartment.

I framed a photo for you of yourself, dark-haired, long sideburns, grinning, holding a golf stick, standing by the Mustang with the cottage by the lake in the background. You looked so pleased with yourself because you had beaten your friend Steve Wennan at golf and he had taken the photo for you. He was a guy your age, a land surveyor, who you had met through work. On Saturday mornings, in the summer, you would pack your golf gear, put on your Dodgers baseball cap and meet Steve for breakfast, always bacon, eggs, muffins and maple syrup and the endless cups of coffee.

We loved Steve's laconic, Southern drawl, so different from the north-east accents. He was from Alabama and lent us a book, *The Truth About Lyndon B. Johnson*, which exposed the corruption of that family and talked about the political intrigues of that man's clawing his way to the presidency. We were fascinated. Government intrigue was not a big issue in political Australian life as we knew it.

The golf matches came to a sudden halt when Steve's wife, a darkhaired, petite Virginian, Susan, left him to become a bikie's moll. She had met some bikies, went with the gang, and walked out on him. He wasn't exciting enough. The life of a surveyor's wife did not fit the picture of life portrayed in the daytime television soaps.

Susan asked me once if I would come to morning tea. The girls were meeting to celebrate the marriage of a couple of characters in *Days Of Our Lives* at 11.15 a.m. on Wednesday. A special cake and champagne were ordered for the celebration. As the couple were married on TV, we would cut the cake and toast their future in champagne. I had to say, 'Yes,' then added, 'What do I wear?' I had a feeling it would not be a jeans and sneakers do.

'We'll all be dressed just like for a wedding.'

Thank God I had asked! I would need to hunt out Aunt Martha's pearls which had come in handy on several other occasions and which had travelled around the world with me in their old satin-backed case.

Steve and Susan lived in a white Cape Cod home in Warwick, with pale blue shutters and a pale blue front door. I walked up the path between manicured lawns feeling more stupid with every clicking step of my high heels, but I couldn't turn back. There they were, all the girlfriends, beautifully dressed and styled, excited, fluttering manicured nails, sitting on the edge of their chairs in front of the television.

'Girls, this is the Australian, Lily.'

It sounded like an exotic food on a supermarket shelf.

'Oh, really! Austria, I just love that country. Sit next to me,' cooed Lucile, her blonde hair sprayed and piled high.

Smiling, uncertain, I nodded, made pleasantries, felt awkward and really weird, as if I was part of a play.

'Oh, Australia, where's that?' demanded Georgia, a real estate agent.

I tried to describe the country I had come from, so close to Indonesia, so far away from America or Europe.

'But you look just like us! Goodness, you're a long way from home. I'm from Minneapolis, that's far enough.'

The TV was announcing *Days of Our Lives*, between Sara Lee advertisements, Kentucky Fried Chicken and soap powder ads.

The wedding episode began. There were tears in the Cape Cod house and hushed silences and appreciative gasps when the bride appeared. I noticed the perfect teeth and masses of hair of the characters who seemed to bounce and flaunt from one crisis to the other within seconds, from smiles and kisses to anger and tears. I wanted to laugh, but instead played with my pearls and drank champagne. I said my thank you, made promises about coming back real soon, and left totally confused.

The lake would be waiting quiet and peaceful after the cacophony of my social christening. I think I understood why Susan grabbed at excitement and an escape from the mindless trivia which seemed to occupy a lot of her time.

I had answered the advertisement for the house to rent by the lake when the lives of other people at the apartment complex were crowding in. We needed some space. It was advertised as a stone cottage set amongst trees with its own pontoon and water supply. It sounded isolated and idyllic.

The days by the lake flowed peacefully, one after the other. I made clothes on an old Singer sewing machine that I had found in the second-hand mill, I painted the letter box purple, I knitted. I wrote poetry and sent letters back to Australia, I went back to university and began my Masters of English Literature, I found that I was pregnant again. That was not the first pregnancy. The Lying-In Maternity Hospital in Rhode Island had many visits from us. The first time had been a desperate bloody dash over icy roads as I lost the first child conceived in Rome. We had been living with Lilly and Ben and had only been in the United States for a month. Ben had pulled his overcoat on over his pyjamas when you had rushed downstairs not knowing what to do. The house was still; everyone was asleep. He had insisted on driving us to the hospital, and as Ben backed the station wagon out onto the street, Tilly insisted on calling Dr Gordon, who said he would meet us at the hospital.

With blood pouring down my legs, I had stood in a red-brown puddle at the reception desk at two a.m. while a large, indifferent black woman drawled out in a dull voice, 'Name, age, nationality, social security number,' so slow, so clear, so loud.

I will never forget Ben's worried face, eyes full of tears behind his thick, round glasses, as he stood with you in the overheated foyer. He stood in his thick brown overcoat, his gloved hands folded, not daring to look at either of us. Both of you were perspiring.

'I am so sorry, so sorry,' he whispered as my face twisted in pain with each cramp. He looked sternly at the woman taking my details and ordered, 'Cut the crap, do something. Now!'

Immediately, she responded, called for two night staff, and I was carried away.

How much safer we felt with Ben. I remember him wearing his hunting cap, his face creased with worry and his voice so concerned. Hospitals are like foreign countries. They have their own cultures, especially a hospital in a foreign country where we had no idea how the system operated.

I had never heard Ben raise his voice in anger before. He is one of the most gentle of men I have ever known who has devoted energy and time to his family, friends and neighbours. He was always incredulous at another man's deceit, cruelty or dishonesty. I think that is why he and Tilly loved the lake as much as we did. It was a refuge for them too.

Both of them were concerned and caring when I came out of hospital a few days later. I lay in bed, listening to the family life below stairs, and watching the bare limbs of the trees outside the window, feeling stripped myself and bare inside. Tilly and Ben were so unhappy for us. There they were with four beautiful children. Tilly would sit on the bed, hold my hands and tempt me with special treats, point out a jaybird on the windowsill, show me her latest knitting. Always gentle. How lucky we were that fate had led us to those special people.

I studied Victorian English literature, taught by a German professor Dr Schwer, who also loved opera. With my discovery of George Eliot, I discovered that I was again pregnant. In the middle of the final exam, I began to miscarry, hurriedly finished my paper and drove myself to hospital. The papers were returned with a comment on mine, 'At this point you seem to lose your concentration,' How could I explain to a bachelor who loved opera that at that point of the exam I was beginning to lose another child?

CHAPTER 18

We have flown back to America six times in the last twenty-five years, three times with Emma. Again we are coming back to see old friends. We fear that time is running out for them. We will be staying again with Ben and Tilly, who have remained dear friends despite the distances and our very separate lives. There is a need to see people, to touch people, to smile and look into the eyes of special friends whose lives we shared. The years have gone too quickly. We are returning because something inside warns that it might be the last time we see them.

Age has not brought peace of mind for them, but ill health and fractured families. Never before have I felt a need to write a journal when I have flown back to America. I have an intuition of lastness, of things changing at a pace I can no longer hold on to. I sense endings.

I will write it all down, the past, the present, the lake, that extraordinary centre of our universe for a few years where we loved, cried, felt lost and angry, belonging but not belonging. I am writing this journal also for Emma, because the lake was the beginning of her world. Wherever she goes, she will have these words to keep the past alive. Whether she wishes to make it her past will be her choice, but it is by the lake that our family began, where she was loved and where she first wondered about the world around her.

I picture these things as we sit in the Dallas airport watching, watching people, the enormous confusion of shapes and colours constantly moving, moving. Australia is so far away. It takes seconds to say, 'I am flying to America.' The reality is flight after flight after flight to reach the east coast of America. One plane to Sydney, one plane to Los Angeles, one plane to the hub, in this case Dallas, one plane to Boston (if not diverted elsewhere by the weather!) Up and down, up and down, up and down, different airports, different flights and the waiting in between.

Tilly has been very ill with heart valve transplants. The family has become fractured and Grandma is dead. There have been divorces and drug addiction and sadnesses that we never dreamed of during those years by the lake.

I remember Tilly and Ben coming with the family for cook outs. You and he would fish in the boat and the kids would scream and leap off the pontoon into the water. Tilly, so gentle and loving, cared for us all. It was Tilly who helped us scrub out the cottage to make it fit to live in, it was Tilly who cared for me during those awful times of losing babies and when Emma was tiny and frail. It was Tilly who introduced me to American supermarkets and that wonderful hamburger joint, Ratties, where we could drive in and order at a post like the drive-in movies. Girls would bring out the order to the car. It was Tilly who cooked Thanksgiving dinners and introduced us to pumpkin pie and baked turkey and ham. Tilly was so pleasant, confident and generous. Who cares for her now?

It is strange putting feet onto the ground and not feel as if they are moving. It reminds me of the time I flew to Australia with my Emma when my mother was ill and we were living by the lake. I knew there was something wrong and had to see her. I'm a person who always acts on the warnings of my instinct.

Tilly had said, 'Go, Lily, go, if that's what you have to do.'

Confused by the horror of the Vietnam war being revealed in America, I felt sick for my brother, a helicopter pilot flying search and rescue missions in Vietnam with the Australian air force. In 1965, Australian Prime Minister Menzies had started sending troops (including conscripts) to Vietnam. We had been told that if we didn't fight in Vietnam it would be Sydney next. It was not until we went to live in London that I found differently and learned the bias of the Australian media.

In 1969, I watched the first man walk on the moon from the safety of the house by the lake. He placed a plaque – 'We came in peace for all mankind'. In November, I watched four Kent State University students in Ohio demonstrating against Vietnam being shot by National Guardsmen. Ten days later, two students were killed at Jackson State College, Mississippi.

The lake at sunset was sometimes apricot-blue. It was easy to see the other side, but I liked it best at sunset, because then the far side of the lake became a dark silhouette and the water took on colours that were not there during the day. There was a softness, a magic that usually made my own spirit still and peaceful. I sat by the lake and wrote a poem for my brother Blake, who I had not seen for seven years.

I Cried For You When You Went To Vietnam
Lake leaves of silent faces floating,
summer of the turtle-time
and salamander sweetness.
No chimes for time but bullfrog bellows
Mark the dark to draw a shroud
Across the lake that hushes, calms,
In satin-singing sleep; wooden fingering
Lattice limbs across a dream for
In the water see the faces floating,
Faces floating in the leaves.
And in this peace is war
And in this beauty blood
And in this silence cries of men
Slow drowning in the dark.
They sent him there to Vietnam
When he was very young.
The blonde, tan boy with surfie bumps
Who quoted Yeats and loved the sun.
He choppered through the orange cloud.
They sent him home a quiet man.
When I sit in armchair warmth
And flaming fire content, I see
the faces flaring, burning faces
in the flames.   *I love you Blake, Lily*

That night, I sat by the fire where smoke had blackened the stone. An antique Italian rifle I had found for you in the Mill sat above the fireplace. I missed my family.

We were living through the American Vietnam agony. No one in America had much idea that Australians were in Vietnam. I knew. My only brother was there. The mailman delivered a letter from my mother. She wrote to say that on Christmas Eve my brother was shown on television, standing beside his Huey helicopter getting ready for a search and rescue mission from the base in Da Nang.

'Your father went to the pub and for the first time in our long marriage he made himself totally blind drunk. We miss you.'

I needed to see my mother and assure her when she saw my baby that there was beauty, that there was life, that she wasn't alone. I ached to see them all.

I told you that I had to go back. It had been almost five years since I had seen my family. I wanted my mother and father to see their granddaughter. I wanted them to have me close by with my brother at war.

America was a distressed country, torn by protesters, injured returning soldiers, television cover that was showing its horrors and the corruption. In January 1968, the Tet Offensive in Vietnam showed the atrocities committed by retreating Vietcong and North Vietnamese.

They killed thousands of civilians suspected of supporting the Saigon government. Americans knew that there were POW's being held in Hanoi. In March of the same year, the massacre of civilians at My Lai in Vietnam's Quang Ngai province horrified Americans. 'Gooks' had caused over one hundred casualties in Charlie Company without them even seeing the enemy, the phantom enemy, with sniper fire and booby traps. They took revenge. Blake had written,

Sis, we don't know who is ally and who is enemy. A woman carrying a load of washing or a kid selling food to us is just as likely to have a bomb hidden and will blow themselves up as well as us. We don't like camping in the jungle with the Yanks. We're

I never got letters from my brother. In all our years of living apart, this
was the first letter he had ever written to me. He was my only brother,
blond and blue-eyed, who had married when I was living in England.
I worried and thought about him.

It would be the first time you and I were to be separated since we
had known each other. I packed a case, said goodbye to the lake, Kitty
and Mac, Ben and Tilly. You drove us up to Boston airport and we
said goodbye. I was not happy to be going. I felt that I was leaving my
security for the unknown. It felt like a goodbye, not an au revoir.

I flew to Los Angeles with Emma for the long flight across America
and then to Australia. We couldn't afford a separate seat for her and at
twenty months she could still travel on my knee. I hoped that the flight
would not be full. I had packed packets of raisins and juice and toys and
disposable diapers and changes of clothes and sedative drops prescribed
by Dr Gordon (who thought that I was mad flying alone that distance
with a small child). I had bought Dr Seuss's *Green Eggs and Ham* (Em
knew it by heart by the time we reached Adelaide, wanted it read over
and over, 'Read Sam I Am, Mum' over and over) and a thick book of
nursery rhymes with rich colour illustrations on thick paper. I thought
of you driving back alone up Ruffstone Road to the lake and an empty
cottage. I had left my safe world and I was nervous.

Sitting next to me on the plane trip from Boston to Los Angeles
was a Californian psychiatrist returning to the west coast after lecturing
at Harvard. He had a shaved, tan head, beautiful teeth and did not
stop talking the entire flight while my small companion wriggled and
squirmed. Paul (we were on first term names ten minutes into the flight)
insisted that we meet his family before we crossed to the International
Terminal. He helped us off the plane and, smiling genially and chatting,

found an airport pusher. His wife, Indian-skirted, jangling jewellery, long, swinging hair, sandalled, smelling of incense, hurried towards him with five children, identically dressed, joined together with dog leads.

I am cautious of psychiatrists.

The Hari Krishna devotees were dancing around and tinkling bells. Machines offered to tell my horoscope if I fed them dollars, dimes and nickels. Another religious group, dressed in white, offered to save me if I and my child went with them and gave them money. It was a relief to reach the international terminal. The flight was called and I lined up to board the Qantas flight to Australia, carrying child and baggage and Blue Rabbit.

By the time we had reached Sydney Airport, I was exhausted. I had sat next to the bulkhead of the plane, where a crib had been fitted. This meant that babies or small children could be laid down to sleep. There were no other facilities in those days for children, no special food, just a few toys, so Emma ate the bottles of Heinz baby pears and yogurt I had packed and drank the formula I had prepared (it seemed so long ago). I had not realised there would be little help for women travelling alone with children.

My greatest fear had been that Em would cry all the way. We were sitting opposite an Indian couple flying to Fiji. Their baby cried and cried. They were embarrassed and exhausted themselves.

There is no escape in a plane. We were stuck there, jammed with hundreds of other people inside a metal tube rocketing through the dark, trying to sleep cramped and bent and uneasy. I could smell the restlessness, the antagonism towards crying children. I read and read aloud until the small blonde head dropped onto my lap and the blue eyes closed until the plane started to drop for landing in Honolulu. Both children screamed, their ears hurting with the pressure of the descent.

Hours later, we were back in the same smelly plane with more passengers clutching their Hawaiian holiday memories. I heard the happy, drawling Australian accent. Mavis and Jack had spent a 'bonzer fortnight', and 'What's the name of your beaut little girl? Yeah, too right, we're from Newcastle.' I wanted to hug them.

I had not seen Sydney Harbour Bridge before, flying into Sydney International. This is Australia! I cried great tears that blobbed onto the cardboard pages of the nursery rhyme 'Jack be nimble, Jack be quick, Jack jump over the candlestick.' If only life was that easy.

Emma clung very tight, sensing my panic. There was no place to change a child on a plane. I could see no place in the airport. We were amongst the last off the plane, so by the time we reached Immigration the lines were long for our passport checks. Baggage collection and Customs had long lines. Sydney Airport was enormous and confusing. I would have to catch a bus to get to the national terminal. Em was wet and uncomfortable and complaining. She too was confused by the noise and the crowds and the movement. I looked down at her sitting in a Qantas pusher and smiled. 'How awful to be so little, so powerless, to have to look up at people all the time and be so totally dependent on someone else.' The thought made me feel brave as I lugged a suitcase, overnight bag, and child in a pusher.

'Is there anywhere I can change a child before I go to the other terminal?' I must have sounded frantic as I asked the woman in a uniform behind the Qantas desk.

'Oh, over there.' She offhandedly pointed in the direction of a hundred people milling through the airport. 'You'll have to leave the Qantas pusher in this terminal.'

'Really?' I was beyond any reasoning, or rational thinking having survived Immigration and Customs, with my legs feeling wobbly with nerves and tiredness.

Furious, I undressed Em, pulled off the soaking diaper and flung it onto the shiny counter.

'Well, you can get rid of this then.'

The supercilious gaze that was an attempt to keep me in my place suddenly crumpled. The pursed pink mouth below the risen plucked eyebrows demanded, 'You can't do that.'

'Watch me.' I changed my child on the shiny counter, popped her back into the airport pusher and with the most defiant swirl I could muster turned my back. Somehow I would need to maintain my calm and control.

Why was I doing this? Why was I putting my child and myself through such awful discomfort and tension? If I had realised what it would be like, I knew I would not have come. The airline had offered a minimum of help and I was now so stressed I was incapable of asking for it.

'Through you go, love. Let me take the luggage and your little girl,' offered a Trans Australian Airline official. 'I'll see you onto the bus and they'll help you at the other end.' It was as easy as that. I was back in familiar territory.

I reached Adelaide, South Australia, after flying from the east coast of America. Flying cattle class is an inhuman form of long travel. Try it with a baby, when airline staff preferred the businessmen with expense accounts and had few facilities for children.

The joy in my parents' faces made the horror of the travel fade. We smiled, we hugged, we cried, I began to relax and realise the importance of my family. Someone had exploded a cracker bomb in my parents' letter box on Christmas Eve after my brother had been shown in Vietnam on the television. I realised the agony that the war was causing in Australia as well and longed to be back by the lake. My loyalties were being torn. Should I stay? Should I go back?

I sat in the kitchen with Mum and Dad, talking about this and that. Mum had sent cuttings with news from Australia and from Adelaide so that I knew in 1968 there had been elections and the Liberals had scraped into power. Australian news seemed dominated by American news. My parents were far more aware of what was happening in America than any American I knew was aware of what was happening in Australia, Asia or the rest of the world. We were living in tumultuous times. I thought of you back by the lake, feeding the ducks when you got home from work. You had written to Em,

Dearest Emma Ann,

I am looking after the ducks and Mouse. The ducks waddle up to the porch, quacking bossily, I think they are looking for you. Then when I take notice of them, they waddle back to the pontoon where they stand and gossip until I deliver the breadcrumbs and scraps. Mum says that you like Grandma's Vegemite and her egg flips. I don't think the ducks would like Vegemite. Once they have clucked thank you, they splash off into the water.

Everyone sends their love and miss you and Mummy. I miss you both most of all. Take care of Mummy. I will see you both very soon.

You are a brave girl flying all that way to Australia in the plane.

Lots and lots and lots of hugs and kisses.

Daddy. xxxxxxxxxxxxxxxxxxxxxxxxxxxxxxxxxxxxxxxxxxxxxxx

Your letter with the forty-two kisses was kept under her pillow. She pretended to read it each night to Blue Bunny. I had to read it over and over until she knew every word by heart.

I had never seen my mother so happy as when she held her first grandchild. Her face glowed. She never stopped smiling. They discovered things together, gum leaves and gum nuts on trees, plums and lemons growing on trees, violets, chooks, shining brass ornaments, letter boxes. I had never seen her like that before and was almost awed by my mother's happiness. She held the round bundle in the red parka as if she might disappear, this small, blonde child unsure of where she was.

With so much love, my child had to grow strong and beautiful.

There were great-grandparents too, my gran and pop in their cottage that had been the only place they had ever lived, a town in the Adelaide hills where they grew apples. Gran, dressed in lavender, her white hair carefully bunned, enclosed me in her soft bosoms, holding me very tight. I never wanted to let go. She was wearing her pearls for this special occasion of meeting her first great-grandchild. Pop, his white shirt, hat and pipe, just as I remembered, was almost blind but could hug and smell the childness of this small person who had come so far to see him. Best sponge, cream puff, chocolate pudding maker in Australia, if not the world, my gran and pop were the focus of my family; the memories of Christmas days with cousins and uncles and aunts came pouring back as we sat around the enormous dining room table.

The freeway to Stirling had just been opened, so had Cleland Park. My parents took Em to introduce her to koalas and kangaroos, driving proudly up the new road. I'd forgotten women wore twinsets and men wore cardigans. Mum had knitted a blue bonnet with a peak and a blue jumper to match Blue Bunny. They were worn everywhere, especially to the park, where she was going to see real koalas and kangaroos like the pictures and toys she had back home by the lake. But this also felt like home.

CHAPTER 19

I had met an old friend who wined and dined me with abandon. He wanted us to stay. His own marriage had failed miserably. I decided to write to you, the most difficult letter I had ever written in my life.

Dearest Pete,

Oh, how I miss you! It's almost three weeks since we left you at Boston airport. Have you gone sailing or fishing or swimming? What is the weather like? How is everyone? I think about you all the time. I listen to my parents in their bed, talking and moving in the dark, and I think of us. I cannot wait for the dawn to break.

I don't know whether it was a good thing to come back. I know that I am happy some days and desperately confused other days. The trip back was hell. Em was wonderful, so very good, but it was hard work for both of us. There is too much of my childhood here in this house for me to feel comfortable and you are not here. I want you so much.

So many strange feelings are choking me. Suddenly, I will see something and remember the past. Our old house at Rose Park opposite the racecourse where I planted a garden full of roses and the almond trees in the backyard.

Remember the huge tree by the garbage can? Remember how we washed walls and made love on that old iron bed. You speared a rat with the iron tip of a curtain rod. I could never look at that fireplace without seeing the rat. But that is past, this is now and when I see the joy in my parents' faces as they hold their granddaughter, I know that I have done the right thing in coming back home.

It doesn't feel like home, though. I don't feel like I belong. I see people from the past and suddenly realise that seven years is a long time. Friends have got on with their own lives and somehow I feel outside of it all. I've seen Jane and Shauna and Don and my grandparents and Kay and Mike, but I know that I will be leaving with our baby so I'm keeping part of me separate. I think it's protection, I don't want to put my roots down too hard, they're sort of sneaking sideways just to give me a hold, but I'm going to have to pull them up and that will hurt when I leave. I don't know what to do. I have met Evan. He is back from England without Sandra. He is being very good to us.

I've spoken to several companies and they are interested in employing someone with your experience, particularly if you had a Masters degree.

There is nothing much available in the universities here in your field of engineering, so that's something we need to talk about when I come back. I will come back, don't worry. Your lonely, loving phone call from the lake made the decision for me. But I do love it here as well. I feel part of the place and there are pieces of me that want to cry, like when I walk on the beach at Port Willunga and watch Em chase the seagulls into the clear water or when I sit by the waterfall at Waterfall Gully with Dad where I picked hundreds of lilies for my wedding. We walked along the creek and it seems like a lifetime ago.

I hadn't realised how much I miss the round Adelaide hills. They're green now. I see them through the window where I slept as a child and where our child now sleeps in a cot painted pink by Dad. In fact, he painted the whole room for his granddaughter, hung pictures, bought toys, a potty chair and a pusher. They haven't stopped smiling since we arrived and Mum has introduced Emma to poached eggs and toast, warm cocoa and all the relatives.

That's the lovely thing about being here. It's the feeling of having real family, generations of it that have lived in the place. Did you know that there's a street in Summertown named after my family? I drove up through the hills with Dad, just him and me, where we used to pick wild orchids when I was a kid near my great-gran's house. I used to think she was the oldest person ever alive, with whiskers on her chin. I used to hate kissing her. How I would love you to hold me and kiss me right now.

I think I have to come back to Australia. Perhaps I'll feel different when I get back to the lake, but I don't think I can deny our parents the happiness and joy I see so clearly now. My parents have suffered enough, with Blake in Vietnam and our absence for so many years. Plus I'm scared to get pregnant again and have to go through it all again, just the two of us, so far away. You know they've told me I can only have one more child. It's too dangerous to do otherwise.

Where do you feel that you belong? Where do you want to live? Do you want to go back to university? Are you missing us terribly?

So many questions. Do you want to become an American citizen?

I've thought about it and I don't think that I want to. I went into the city to meet Evan for lunch and I loved the feel of the place. I caught the bus. It was clean, full of matrons with gloves and bags who smiled and chatted and students going to the university. The shops and the streets were so clean. There are even neighbours around here who I have known since I was a child who chat and go ga-ga over Emma. I think what I am trying to say is that even though I'm feeling separate and different in many ways, I want to belong.

This is scary. I belong with you, in our house by the lake. I belong where so many of our friends have sheltered and loved us, but I belong here too. I'm afraid. I don't know what to do. I can't talk to anyone about it. No one else here is in that position. They all seem to be comfortably fixed and purposeful, seem to know who they are. I don't know any more.

I'm writing this letter to you, this crazy pouring out, while I'm sitting under the apple tree in the backyard. The apple tree that I painted, the first oil painting that I sold. See what I mean? The connections keep oozing out all the time. This makes me think of this, makes me think of that.

I don't have that in America, only when I'm with you.

I'm booked on Qantas flight 937 to LA out of Sydney on 10 August, then Continental F37 to Boston. We'll fly straight through, so will probably be in a mess when you see us. I'll be back for our wedding anniversary. (I'll pack a bottle of Henschke's Riesling for us to drink by the lake.) I've bought a few pairs of Australian men's shorts, too – short shorts, not those awful things the Yanks call shorts that hang around your knees and droop behind. Aussies call them baggy britches.

I can't wait to see you. I imagine you here at night, and I am feeling your body that I know so well. I wish you were here. We always talk things over together and you're not here to do that. You are my very best friend as well as my lover and the father of my child. You are very precious. I do love you so much. We have a lot to talk about, many decisions to make.

When I lay alone in the hospital, wondering if Em would live or die, wondering about my own recovery, I so desperately longed for my family. I never said anything, but if only my mother, father or my brother had walked through the door, I think the awful heaviness and responsibility would have been lifted. You and I have carried everything alone for many years. When the parcels of hand-knitted baby clothes started to arrive from Australia and the cards from aunts and uncles and friends, with their loving messages, and the infant kangaroo boots and the toy koalas, I think I knew then that I would have to return to Australia. It stirred something very deep that I had not wanted to acknowledge. Now I have to confront it and say, 'This is what I want.' It may not be what you want.

I will see you very soon, my darling. The time is passing quickly.

Twenty-eight days are passing in a flash (though the night times are dreamless and endless and the bed is cold and lonely). Some of our friends are not very happy. They have come back to Australia after years away and have not adjusted to the changes. It's that feeling of once you're back, you're back and there's no escape. Adelaide is small and comfortable, people are pretty self-satisfied and don't want to know where I've been or what I've done. It's an 'I'm OK. Thank you, don't disturb.' So somehow, if we do come back, we'll have to search out where we belong, If we belong. I am saying, we.

I wish you could be sharing all this stuff with me. Don't be angry when I say how I feel. I know you find it very hard. It must be awful for you alone, and reading this. But at least you will know what is happening inside me before I come back.

My feelings for you have not changed. I was scared that they would, that I would begin to think about you differently. But I have grown up.

I have had to make decisions by myself. You and Em are the most important people in my life. I am returning to you because it is the decision I have made.

I love you

Lily

My mother never recovered from that time. When Blake flew in from Vietnam, my father was up north at a mine. He was caught in a cyclone and couldn't return to meet his son at the airport, so my mother went alone. Blake's uniform was hanging on him, as he had lost so much weight. His face was haggard and old beneath his smile. He went to church with my mother on the Sunday, wearing his air force uniform to the church where he went to Sunday school as a child.

'Not a person spoke to him,' she wrote. 'He came home, took off his uniform with his medals and took them up to the burner. He set fire to them when he found out about the explosion in the letter box. He says he can't live in Australia. He's not wanted, none of the Vietnam veterans are wanted. He's going to get his wife and go to Singapore.' She would smile when I saw her two years later, but only her lips would move. Everyone my mother loved left her. My father was never there when she needed him.

I had taken photos, so many photos. They would not replace the hugs, the closeness, the need for roots and belonging. But at least I would have photos. My brother had gone. I would not see him for many more years when we would meet in Kuala Lumpur. He is my only living relative now and still we are thousands of miles apart. I love him but know so very little about him as a man. There is an emptiness inside me when I think about those years.

My father said when I cried about leaving to go back to you and our life by the lake, 'Pickles, you made your bed, you lie on it.'

That is cruel. It still makes me feel lonely and disconnected and guilty.

As we board yet another plane and I open my journal to write about our past and the lake, my mind goes back to when I boarded the flight, leaving my parents to return with my child to you, waiting in America by the lake in Greenville. It proved to be the saddest flight I have ever made and I feel the tears as I write this years later. The plane was full of American soldiers returning from Vietnam. Some had been spending time on R and R in Sydney before returning home, and others had met their families who had been flown to Sydney and were returning to America together. The plane was so heavy with emotion that I felt it had to crash. I was full of trepidation and doubts about my own return, but they were swallowed by a sadness I felt all around me.

Some men were bandaged, some had eyes that were wild and hysterical, loud voices. The women were quiet, confused, desperately smiling, trying to understand. Some men clutched at them, groping, crying, others sat cut off, quiet, unable to share private nightmares as their women tried to break through the shield. The women were bewildered, with downcast eyes. Their men had been through experiences they could never share, but they had suffered the taunting and the horrible anger of the protesters at home. I smiled into the eyes of some of the women, who smiled back with quivering lips. Their men would not, could not be reached. Others became blind drunk. I shrank into my corner seat, crooning to my child. Those eyes will always haunt me.

We fastened seat belts for the descent to Boston. Gradually, the whirring of the plane's landing receded in my head and I looked through the window. Would you be there? Would you still look the same as a month ago.

'Daddy will be there, Daddy will be there,' I had repeated and repeated like a desperate mantra. 'Please, please be there!'

What would you look like? What would you be wearing? What would your eyes be saying? I couldn't wait to get out from this smelly metal tube that had incarcerated us since we had left Adelaide.

Emma was agitated. 'Daddy, I want my daddy, he'll be here,' she instructed Blue Bear, lying exhausted in her arms, his ears bent and tangled.

This time, an air hostess helped me bundle our hand luggage together. Nowhere else in the world do people stuff so much hand luggage into a plane. They demand to bring amounts on board that would make Australian flight crews apoplectic.

'It's their constitutional right,' I muttered to no one in particular.

We were both so tired. My child's eyes were wide open with tiredness, my head was pounding. Would you like the way I looked? Would you be happy to see us? A month can be a lifetime when so much has happened in between. I had gone to Australia with our child to see her grandparents, I had flown to see my parents who were so unhappy with my brother in Vietnam. The plan had seemed so easy. The reality had proved devastating. Now I wanted to return to

Australia with you because I had felt something that you could not share. Somehow, I would have to make my feelings known and shared, otherwise I would have to go alone. After the years together and by the lake, I shuddered at the thought. Neither of us was free. We had a child.

I wanted to go back to Australia, I knew it so clearly as Em's hot, small hands clung to mine. My feet echoed, go back, go back, go back, so loud that I found it hard to concentrate on her chatter down the long walk to the terminal.

'I can show Daddy all the pictures of grandmas and grandpas and old pop and ninny.'

'You certainly can, my darling.'

Mothers' minds work at so many levels, they are like layered Napoleon cakes. I wanted to return. I knew it, I had told no one, it was a thought filling my head. I would have to pick the right time. We would have to be alone, together.

Em saw you first. You looked thin and worried, then your face broke into a great, happy grin. I saw your smile and knew that whatever happened, I would never forget that smile, or such joy, such unguarded happiness. A smile I would treasure for a life time.

'It's Daddy!' Em. broke away and was off, heading towards you, small legs trotting fast.

You bent to pick her up, enfolding her as she collapsed into your long arms. The arms that held me, that threw baseballs, and cast fishing lines, that chopped wood for our fires, that raked leaves in Fall, that held newspapers firmly with the occasional, annoyed twitch, that held bunches of violets bought for me.

How is it possible that so much can race through the mind in seconds? Decisions can be made in an instant that will affect lives for generations.

You held us both so tight. You had been afraid that we would not return to you and our life by the lake. You were afraid that there was someone else from the past who would hold me from returning.

Unbeknown to me, Evan had phoned you from Australia to tell

you just that. 'They will not be returning. They're staying here with me,' he had said.

We had been friendly with him and his wife when we all lived in London. He had returned to Australia without her. I had met him and he had talked about the sadness of his divorce and his loneliness and how he missed old friends. He had adored Emma, flattered my mother and pleaded with me to stay. He said that he had always wanted me, but that you had always been there. I had begun to shake all over. All of the emotions I had controlled over the last years seemed to explode.

I wept in front of him until I could not see or breathe and my eyes were black smudges of melting mascara that dripped all over my fancy white shirt. I sniffled and borrowed his handkerchief to wipe my nose and my eyes. I refused to sleep with him. He was not you.

He never told me that he had phoned you and invaded our private world by the lake. You never told me until weeks later after I had returned that he had phoned, that he had mocked you, told you you had lost your wife and child to him. But we had come back to you. There had been no choice as far as I was concerned. We had shared too much, had suffered too much together.

'I missed you so much. I was frightened you wouldn't come back. You're home, it's all right.'

Where was home? I hid my face in your shoulder so you couldn't see my eyes.

We drove the back way from Boston once we had cleared the ring route from the airport. The weather was glorious and balmy. I wanted to look at you, hold your hand, wipe away your frown. You were so quiet.

The trees on either side of the road had become a gaudy canopy of flaunting orange and yellow. This was our fifth autumn season in North America. Fall was like a carnival celebration of nature, a defiant explosion of colour before the white of winter. Trees were covered in burning red leaves against grey branches and a blue sky. The ground was a carpet of red. Every plant seemed to burn with colour. We drove past white wooden churches with white belfry towers above steep-pitched rooves. Churches surrounded by graveyards with grey burial stones. The white made them look centres of innocence, but I'm not convinced. There is so much intrigue within churches. And they had burned women as witches up in this area. Perhaps that is why the leaves of trees turn blood red in the fall against the white buildings of men. Nature's wake for the dead.

We drove through the New England countryside, so different from the place I had left. I thought of the sombre, olive coloured droop of gum leaves, already resenting the brazenness of colour surrounding us. My parents had a frangipani in a tub by the front door. By the lake we had dogwood and rhododendron. Emma was asleep in the back of the car. We said little to each other.

Was it Conrad who said, 'Home is where the heart is?' I had to search inside and find that answer. When you have lived away from your own country, but also love another place, it must be like having a mistress. The tenderness, the comfort of what is known and the excitement, the risk of what is unknown and to be discovered.

I haven't thought of that before. The restlessness becomes panic sometimes when I feel that I will never belong anywhere.

CHAPTER 20

You must have been burning leaves before driving up to Boston, I could smell them as we turned into Ruffstone Road. We carefully placed Em in her cot and kissed her as she muttered and sighed, clutching for Blue Bunny. As she curled onto her side, I watched your face as you turned towards me.

'Is this where you really want to be? I want you, I will have you.'

I shuddered all over, silently pleading that you understand. I don't know. I want to be with you, I want the three of us together, but I don't know where. I want to go home. This isn't home.

When you touched me, it was like an electric shock. How hungry we were for each other as we lay by the fire. We made love with desperation, almost panic. Our bodies, moulded together, would solve any problem. Savage kisses, breasts pressed hard against your firm body, I didn't have to think. Bodies are separate things, but when they are locked together, the thinking can come later.

'We have to talk,' you murmured.

I had fallen asleep all the afternoon and the night.

You were up, had emptied the cases, bathed Em and fed her and Mouse. 'Would you like a coffee?'

The washing machine was churning away in the basement, everything was back to normal. Everything was different.

'I feel revolting. Let me have a bath and I'll feel better. Is Em OK? Oh, it's so good to see you. I missed you. I've brought back some shorts and some passionfruit pulp. I'll make you a pavlova.' My tongue was running away with me. I was embarrassed in front of my own husband, so much seemed to have happened to separate us.

'Mouse got stuck up a tree. I had to call the fire brigade to come and get him down, he was up so high and wouldn't move. I think he was looking for you and Em.'

'I went to Port Willunga. We walked on the beach. It was so beautiful.'

Our woven pattern of understanding each other's unspoken words was disjointed. The old familiarities, unfamiliar. It would take time. Our bodies knew each other, were passionate, but the words, they were stilted and guarded. The water from the lake slapped at the supports of the pontoon with exactly the same rhythm as it had always done, the sun set with the same different beauty every night, the ducks quacked their same, bossy messages. We were a family again.

During the weekend, we raked and burned, soft charcoal mist rising from the red flames eating piles of brown, brittle leaves. It was good to have something to do together. Emma fed the ducks, tumbled in the piles we raked, and talked to Mouse and her toys, all her gossip from Australia. She was a talker, who loved words, just like her mother.

You and I eyed each other, wary of what had happened to separate us. Evening after evening, the sunsets became our meeting place when you returned from work. We became familiar with each other's talk again, against the background of the lake and the setting sun. The trunks of trees silhouetted like a black lattice against the sun are recurring images in my mind. I return to the lake wherever I am. The horizon, a soft gold spreading as far as I can see. The other side of the lake a black silhouette behind the sun which has fallen orange into the water.

Its reflection spreads in golden ripples, the water is gold. The sky slowly turns pale indigo purple as night falls. In this place, we came to know each other again and decide on the future for the three of us.

CHAPTER 21

'If I go back to university, I'll need to get a scholarship. You won't be able to earn enough, and we have a child.' You were adamant. University meant that we would have to travel somewhere else for a postgraduate degree.

'There are companies in Australia who are interested in you if you go back to university in America. I've got the addresses and the phone numbers for you to contact.' I had been shrewd.

'We'll be below poverty level income if you can't work where we go. Can you manage that?' I thought you were almost hostile.

'If we don't do it now, you'll never get another chance. These Masters degrees aren't available in Australia.' I was cajoling.

'What about you? What will you do?'

'Well, Em is still little. There's no child care we can afford. I'll see if I can get some work in the Communication Skills area in the university.' I was positive.

'We'll need to go somewhere warm. The food will be cheaper, we won't have heating bills and we won't need as many clothes. Down south, if I can get a place.' Your engineering practicality had taken over. You liked the idea.

'Do you want to go? What's your future here? We'll have to take out American citizenship if we stay.' I was gushing it all out. 'Nothing stays still in this life. And you haven't been back to Australia. Things are really different there now from when we left.'

Slowly, slowly, we talked it through, becoming more excited and not really realising the changes that would be involved. No more lake, no more aspen trees, no more sunsets on the water, no more Wordsworth cottage. And what about our special friends? We had woven people into the very essence of who we were in our life by the lake. But I had changed. You knew that. I thought that I knew what was best for the three of us.

'What about Emma?' you asked quietly.

We looked at our busy little girl, always so busy. What did she want? This was her home, the only home she had known, except for the hazy collection of whirlwind experiences and a confusion of faces from the month in Australia. How do you find out from a two-year-old what is important, what they want?

There was a bond between you and Emma. You seemed to intuitively fit each other's actions and expressions. It was a delight to see you together, laughing, chasing, whispering secrets, your faces touching. We had taught our daughter affection and laughter and she trusted people. We had to keep that laughter and trust secure. We had never treated her as an infant, but as a small person who understood things and who deserved respect and sharing.

Ben and Tilly, their children, Mac and Kitty, they were her family. How could we take her away from the security of their love and just their being there doing all the normal things that had become part of the routine of our lives? It would be a wrenching break for us and them. What would it be like for her?

'Don't underestimate her,' you warned. 'She's a survivor, she likes people, she's curious. Nothing is forever. If things don't work out, we'll come back.'

You were lying. We knew there would be no return once we had left.

I talked to Em about going away on a long trip to where the sun shone a lot and that she would see her grandmas and grandpas and koalas and kangaroos later on. Daddy was going to go to a big school so that he could learn things that people needed in Australia. We would go with him to help him. He would need our help. We were his special girls.

Em became clinging, needing reassurance and attention, as

she helped me begin to pack. We were going to a huge campus in Texas which had awarded you a scholarship and we were going to take a minimum of stuff with us. The Mustang would be dragging a U-Haul van as we made our way south. The decision had been made irrevocable when the landlord decided that he would do up the cottage and use it himself. I think he wanted to feel part of what we had shared with him in his house. Emily and Howie Bradley took Mouse.

CHAPTER 22

We are stuck in a smelly plane in Memphis Airport because no air traffic is being allowed into Boston. It is April 1997 and below freezing but no one will say if it is snowing, sleeting or raining in Boston. This plane is safe, it is full of returning business men and women punching away at their laptop computers, or making phone calls or polite chat with a neighbour over a Scotch or diet Coke. They are putting in more fuel in case there is a problem after take-off and Boston is closed again. It is the size of everything that amazes, the numbers, hundreds of planes, thousands of people, phones in the plane which people are using now to phone ahead and warn of late arrivals. It all works. We've just taxied across a road, the runway is a bridge. (And they're making such a parochial fuss in Adelaide about doing the same thing. How little and comfortable and self-important the town of my birth seems from here.) Here, they just do it.

As we fly or sit in airports, I am reading Gertrude Stein's *Everybody's Autobiography*. She is often incomprehensible and boring yet calls herself the most important writer of writers. It was her brother who began the collection of French art in the twenties. Would she be able to trumpet her literary place if she had stayed in America and not joined the expat American literati in Paris? She lived and wrote dangerously.

I wonder what my life would have been like if I had stayed in America? She makes me think about this as the plane purrs towards Boston through a blue sky. Forget might-have-beens. The middle-aged woman who looks back at me in the small window has no regrets. Well, perhaps a few.

I think of illusions. Life is full of them. They make the reality so much more bearable.

New England – Boston, that is – is dark and grey as we fly in. It is raining, cold, and everyone is wearing coats and it feels very New England. Our old friends, Ben and Tilly, are once more gentle and hospitable. They are waiting for us as we drive into their street in a car we have hired in Boston. How quickly we fall back into sensing the right routes to take and the right streets to get to their house.

Thirty years does not seem so long ago. It is bewildering how time can pass with such silent, insidious speed. Our friends are aged with hurts and disappointments. The golden son stole their silver, gathered over the years, wears dirty jeans, wears his red hair in a ponytail and rides a bike because he has lost his licence. My friend does not want to look at him, speak to him, touch him. This was the angel child whose father now gets up at six-thirty every morning to collect him for work to ensure that he at least makes an appearance. He is a good craftsman with wood, but can't hold down a job. I used to read to him when he was a small boy. The daughter, who married a thirty-year-old in a fourteen-year-old body, takes all the responsibilities for her two boys, works full time and pays all the bills. The husband has left to live with his young secretary, but comes home to be fed a good meal and to see the boys. When she is with her parents, she becomes the laughing, easy-natured girl I remember helping to rake leaves under the trees at the lake. There are two other sons. The eldest has become seriously successful and ambitious. The other has taken on a second job to pay for his wife's bills, with her breast implants and her capped teeth and her demand for fun and freedom. She wants more money to spend and hides from her husband's born-again Christianity in her Portuguese Catholicism. You remember them as laughing, playing children, chasing chipmunks by the lake.

Once again, we are sleeping in the bed we first shared when we came to America, wondering what on earth we had done, when I was first pregnant. The black limbs of the oak trees are latticed against the pale blue sky as I look through the window. It will be a fine day. The threat of snow is gone but it is still cold. I am in bed, content and warm, not in a hurry to do anything except listen to my pen. I am reminded of so many years ago when, warm and contented, we lay in the double bed in our timber-lined bedroom upstairs by the lake, the limbs of the aspen trees latticed against the sky. Emma was asleep and we had made love.

How I loved your body, so firm and strong. Just the sight of each other naked and we would have to touch each other. We had made love in the piles of autumn leaves we had raked together, we had made love on the hard wood of the pontoon after a naked midnight summer swim, we had made love on the white reindeer pelt by the fire in winter, heady from mulled wine. Like Lady Chatterley, I had covered you in Lily-of-the-Valley in Spring and we had made love until the bed collapsed in the middle and we sprawled, naked and giggling. We know each other well.

There had been a knock on the door. Reluctantly, you had dragged on a T-shirt and a pair of jeans and gone to open the door.

'Good God, Leonard. How did you find us? What are you doing here?'

'I looked for you in Canada. I found you'd come to America. So here I am.'

'Well, come in. Lily, it's Leonard!'

'Len, fantastic! Come in, come in! Where have you been? Are you hungry? Coffee? How long can you stay?' I had dragged on a jumper and a pair of track pants. I didn't know whether my old college friend would recognise me, I was now streaked blonde, not the long brown haired skinny woman he had seen in Europe over four years ago.

Leonard and I had been friends at Adelaide University in South Australia. We had worked together on magazines and publications for three years until we had gone our separate ways after graduation. Then, later, we met again, very unexpectedly. Len was a small, wiry man with a large nose, wide smile and olive skin. He was a funny man, with a quick wit and able to work through problem situations calmly. But he was the last person I expected to meet face to face when we were on the Greek island of Ios so many years ago.. The man who was walking towards me down the only paved street of the island of Ios in fitted the description of my old friend.

'Len?'

'Lily?'

In that instant of recognition, we clutched and we hugged, then he fainted at my feet. The only time a man has ever fallen at my feet. However, it wasn't that he was overcome. He had fainted from hunger.

Len said that he had been wandering Europe for years, picking up jobs, but always broke. He hadn't eaten properly since leaving the island of Skiathos, so we fed him up, swapped news and gossip, then went our separate ways. I told him that when we returned to Australia I would contact his parents and tell them he was OK.

Yanni, who saw everything, sitting in the sun outside his son's taverna, chortled and called us over. He sat every day in his striped pyjamas which a son had sent from America, reading that son's letters over and over.

'Children, remember. Mountains never meet like people.' Here was Len, standing in the door way of our house at the Bonneville Lake in Rhode Island, America.

You quizzed, 'You're not going to faint?'

'Oh, no. I was hoping I could stay for a few days. I've got a job in the Berlitz School in Mexico City. To teach English. Thought I'd look you up on the way.'

Leonard went out with you to cut wood, did a bit of gardening, cooked sometimes while I washed and ironed his few clothes from his backpack. He was an easy man to live with, never imposing, funny and with so many stories from the places he had been.

'You live in an Eden here,' he commented, but his stories were as unsettling as the fatal apple, his tales were as tempting as the serpent's hiss. He had become an adventurous traveller who felt that he did not belong anywhere in particular any more. 'I stay where my suitcase fits under the bed,' he joked.

But I sensed a lostness in him. He had no intention of returning to Australia planning to wander wherever fate led him.

I resented him a little for making me feel restless, he seemed so peaceful and accepting. He had a special love for children and would spend hours with Em. He fed her in her high chair, made funny faces on empty eggshells, painted his fingers and played finger puppet games, sang, 'Incy Wincy spider climbed up the water spout' (with actions), until we were all singing it in our sleep, made bubble pipes and blew bubbles with washing-up liquid until she screamed in delight. We ran around trying to catch ephemeral rainbow bubbles that soared across the water or burst into the trees.

Even the ducks liked Len. They quacked as he and his small companion concentrated on naming them all – Sara, Sam, Becca, Claude, Bertha – but I never was sure who was who, although they seemed to know. Len happily quacked and flapped around sending the ducks into a frenzy and Em into hysterics.

He loved the lake. But not the water; would not venture into a small boat, often sitting by the water's edge, quiet and still.

'Where are you, Len?' I wanted to ask, but never did.

We had only scratched the surface of knowing about each other and that is the way he wanted it. Every person needs his space, Len more than most. I never interrupted him and kept Em away when he was like that. Len was a loner. He told of his travels but that is all he told about himself. I don't think he knew who he had become without the drug of travel. The laconic humour, the off-handed put-downs of himself, hid an insecure man.

That is why he loved children and had such instant rapport with our child. He could entertain and be asked no searching questions. I did not inquire.

After three weeks or so, he kissed and hugged us goodbye, promising to keep in touch. We drove him to the Greyhound bus station in Providence and gave him the names of friends in Texas.

Letters occasionally dropped in to the mailbox with exotic stamps from Mexico. He was living with three girls from the Berlitz School and teaching English. He loved Mexico but wanted to move on. The last letter delivered to the lake said that he was going down the Amazon. He had posted it from Bogota.

Leonard was found with his throat cut in the seedy part of Brazil's capital. The news of his death appeared in a small column of an Australian newspaper four years after we had waved him goodbye.

How do you explain the passing of time and accept it with grace. I can hear Tilly and Ben in the kitchen below, talking to you. You are the restless one too. You are up and showered and have brought me a cup of tea. You are ready to conquer and make the most of another day.

Except for the different wallpaper and curtains, it is as if we have stepped back into the past, to the first time when we stayed with our friends in 1967. Now it is thirty years later and I like it in this still quiet place, not having to go anywhere or do anything special. Except memories of the past keep flooding back. Tilly and Ben still live in the same house in Massachusetts, now with a swimming pool, dozens of bird feeders, grandchildren and retirement.

I enjoy being alone with space and quiet by myself after planes and airports and crowds of people. I no longer find it exciting, no longer tingle with the thrill of travel. The end now justifies the means. You and I get on well, talk together, share our feelings and our thoughts, but there have been tired, irritable times in our recent close encounters when tempers have been stretched tight and voices have been sharp and critical.

We all have our worlds that occasionally meet, but most times we are all separate and alone creatures. Accepting this keeps me strong. If you can share anything with another person and glimpse a soul, then that is rare and precious. The lake was where we shared and revealed pieces of our souls to each other. That is why it is one of the most precious places to me. We faced life and death in that place, but the lake 'holds what's passing and forgets the past'. Our lives by the lake were not reflections.

CHAPTER 23

The great Dane and the long-legged redhead emerging from the two-man tent in the Maine camping ground were certainly not what they seemed. We had left the lake and Ben and Tilly were looking after Emma for a few days while we went camping along the New England coast. They had decided that I looked pale and tired and needed a change somewhere different, while Tilly was looking forward to having our baby for a few days of mothering after her fall into the lake.

We were having our fill of clam chowders and whitewashed wooden houses and cranberry bogs and small fishing harbours. It was the first time we had been separated from our child and we were anxious.

The camping ground was lush and green with hot showers, but the nights were cold. I looked at the small blue tent and the enormous coffee-coloured dog. Then, at the woman who was emerging after it.

Her red hair was down to her waist and swinging either side as she picked up sticks for a campfire. Then the dark-haired, hawk-nosed man stepped out from under the flap.

'Devious creature, it's all in your mind,' you chuckled and dug me in the ribs. 'Let's make a fire and boil the billy. We can heat up that chowder.'

I went to the ablution block to fill the kettle with water at the same time as the redhead.

'Hi.'

'Hello, I'm Lucy. Where are you from?'

'Rhode Island. Actually, we're Australian.'

'Hey, didn't think you sounded like a New Yorker.'

'I'm just getting water for the billy.'

'What's that?'

'Water to boil to make a cuppa.'

'What's a cuppa?'

'Come and share one with us and you'll find out.'

'OK. Sounds great. See you in ten. We'll bring marshmallows to toast.'

So we met Lucy and David, Cloe the dog and, much later, Jonathon the baby. Lucy wove textiles and David wrote to his father in Shakespearean sonnet form. They came often to stay by the lake. We spent nights by the fire talking philosophy, politics, the rights and wrongs of the Vietnam war until the early hours of the morning and the sun would be coming up over the lake. I thought of them as special, separate friends. We wrote poetry to each other and went to stay in their old wooden house in East Hampton, Massachusetts, the house with the outside stairs where a woman who had been accused of witchcraft had been dragged down to her inquisition and torture.

We visited them in summer, driving the Mustang in the fine, light evening. How much thinner I was. Your hair was long and dark and thick, while mine had been bobbed. My legs were long with skinny knees beneath a green miniskirt. We sat outside and drank Mateus, listening to Pueblo Indian flute music, determining that one day, before we died, we'd go to New Mexico together. Together we went to a factory outlet and bought floral jeans and coloured jackets. We saw lobster pots piled in pyramids on the wharf near Maine when we went camping with them in the Arcadia National Park, where the showers were hot and clean and the tent sites grassed and level.

David composed flute music but we also knew the words of 'Isabella', 'Eskimo Blue Day', 'Let the Sunshine In' and all the Beatles' songs. David and Lucy had been to Woodstock! We felt part of an important world. The lake seemed to draw people. It was like being in a permanent holiday place. When they came to stay, you and David went fishing on the lake for big-mouth bass. He bought you a Pike Chubb Pikie lure, an enormous wood carved fish with savage hooks that has travelled the world and now hangs above the kitchen sink. It has never been used for fishing, but makes a great decoration. You might never have caught anything with it, but what a delicious name and what great memories it stirs whenever I wash the dishes.

David and Lucy moved to New York. In our own movings to so many other places, we eventually lost their address, but I still have the photos of their boys, because they had written to tell us they had adopted an abandoned black baby. We wrote to each other for many years. I would love to see them again.

That is America. People meet and move and meet and move. It is a nation of people constantly on the move. Three years is a long time to stay in one place.

But we cannot return. I realised this most powerfully when we called in to see our old landlord, the son of the man who had built the house by the lake. Thin, funny, he had been married to a beautiful blonde woman with exquisite taste and gentle ways. He had adored her and their three children. Ten years ago, she had died from cancer and his world had begun to crumble. He had married his young secretary quickly. We will not see him again, although you and he had enjoyed some good times together.

We knock on the door. A man opens it whom neither of us recognise. Our spunky landlord of so many years ago has become bloated, unshaven, uninterested, wearing a jacket over a whitish singlet, is barefooted. He is divorced from the secretary, sees little of his children, makes overhead enclosures for swimming pools and lives on junk food.

We have nothing in common and say goodbye.

In fact, it is getting close to the time we must once again say goodbye and fly to Australia. I'm raking oak leaves on the lawn of our friends' house, picking up sticks and branches torn down by the last unseasonal snowstorm, just as we used to do by the lake. It is a rhythmic, regular, thoughtless activity and I am enjoying it. Everybody is outside today working in gardens, walking and looking at other people's gardens. It is one of the first sunny New England days. Everyone has a new rake or broom or leaf collector.

It is a great day for shopping. It is still the great American leisure occupation. It is an entertainment, the acquisition of things and eating food, great quantities of food and great waste. I know it used to shock me so many years ago. The shopping malls are secure, well lit, comfortably decorated and patrolled. What better way to spend a few weekend hours, burn the credit card and acquire more things. Most Australians would thoroughly approve. We have become so American in many ways.

Everything is big and generous, just as I remember it, like so many of the people. One teabag makes two cups of tea, one ice cream cone is huge enough for two, one plate of hamburger satisfies the hunger of two. There are so many of everything in this country, so many rivers, so many mountains, so many cities, so many highways. So much of everything, even the Spanish onions are three times the size of anything I have seen before. The Californian oranges have peel which folds off with each segment equal and large.

The people are large, tall that is, but many are fat, not just round but fat, yet there are shops for petites. Tilly is petite, our landlord's wife was petite, Francine was petite, so they must be around but I don't see many. When you live in a place and become a local part of the life, you don't notice much at all after a while. It's only when you come back from being outside that the differences strike.

Americans outside of New York are mostly polite, that's nice, and there is civic pride in the suburbs where I notice that the streets and sidewalks are clean (unlike the freeway verges now the snow has melted). They drink hard liquor here, Bloody Marys, daiquiris, screwdrivers, not one but often three or four. I can't see any warnings, 'Drink, don't drive!' or 'Speed Kills'. If people are fools, they suffer the consequences. In Australia, I think, we are cocooned and protected from ourselves in a way that astonishes Americans.

There are good things about such a system, but I see people are far more dependent on handouts and aggressive about what they are owed in Australia than I have observed in many other places. It is hard to create the right social balance. There seem to be the disgustingly rich and the poor wherever I look. The stretch limousine delivering the wealthy drug dealers to the door of a swanky New York hotel, where their diamonds glint, glides past the bag lady who sleeps over the hot air vents in the side alley. This is as sickening as the dole exploiters who consider it their right to surf every day in the Queensland sun while they collect unemployment payments, as they have done for three generations. 'It is our right,' they say.

The shingles, the azaleas, the daffodils, hyacinths and tulips are all shiny. It is a sunny day in April. The trees are beginning to green in the few days we have been here. We walk past beautiful homes with gables, shutters, breezeways, manicured lawns, pink, lavender, dark blue woodwork and not a single galvanised-iron shed. Sheds in Australia are utilitarian and ugly, where cars rest and men hide to do their men things.

Here, men hide in the basements to work with hammers, chisels, nails and wood. Garages are an architectural extension of the house.

The houses might be beautiful but, like bandages, they are holding together families often in a state of change or dissolution. All the stuff of American television melodrama is here and the people watching TV must surely realise that often it is their own lives being portrayed in flashing moments. But the houses are beautiful with spring wreaths on the doors and spring flags hanging on flagpoles in the gardens to welcome the new season. The last time we were here, the flags being flown were the American stars and stripes. They have given way to pansies and daffodils, in New England anyway. We watch Cadillacs and Thunderbirds, Lincolns, Continentals, sleek, beautiful cars gliding out of driveways.

Our Mustang would be a heap of wrecker's yard junk by now.

CHAPTER 24

We are indulging in my favourite fat food of America, Dunkin Donuts, before we pack and go to Newport for a picnic with our friends. Then we will take one last nostalgic trip to the lake. To confirm that it is still there, but to also refresh the special memories so that we can tell Emma.

We sit on a rug on the public beach in the shadow of a burnt-out mansion, watching kites fly and eating ham and cheese rolls. We walk around the base of the burnt stone walls, looking at the foundations of huge rooms. Were we standing in the stables? Was this the ballroom with the massive fireplaces at each end? I imagine that I hear laughter, Gatsby men and women dancing the foxtrot, drinking, smoking, using long, ebony holders. Tilly reminisces, 'Ben and I danced in the ballroom of the Elms. Years ago. It was the grandest thing I've ever done. I wore a green, strapless ball gown, silver sandals and had my hair especially done.'

'She looked beautiful,' grinned Ben. 'And I had a full head of hair and could dance like a dream.'

While the memories are so vivid, the past can never be reduced to ruins like the ones we are standing in. The wonderful times help us build again onto disappointments and sadness.

I wonder about the wealth, the incredible wealth that built these mansions and maintained lifestyles where money was no object.

I watch a young woman in red track pants and T-shirt run with a kite. Every piece of her body is bouncing, her face is red and exhausted by the effort. She is laughing and everyone watching her is smiling at her joy and pleasure. She makes me feel happy.

Ben suggests that money would never have been thought about, ever, in this place. It would never have been valued because there was no need.

The cliff walk in Newport, on this cold, spring day, takes us past huge, grand homes. They represent the millions of dollars possessed by people who lived utterly indulged lifestyles, who always thought the money would be there. Wealth. That is so very American. The replica Versailles with turrets, the Hotel Viking on the Avenue of the Mansions, with its Vanderbilt and Garden rooms, Bailey's Beach, the private beach of the elite, as are Hazard's Beach, Easton Beach and Goosebury Beach. All beyond our reach. They never were within our reach.

We walk past the Breakers, built in 1895, the summer house of Cornelius Vanderbilt. We have seen the ornate slate dining room, the eighteenth-century reception room, the great hall, the kitchen full of enormous hanging copper pots that reflect like polished suns, and all I can think of this time is 'Who cleans them?' It is a place of a glamorous past and I am glad we have come again to feel the ghost of it. Now, I feel no awe.

I remember when you and your brother drove me to Newport down snowy roads, where bare branches hung white and heavy. You had brought me home from hospital two days before Christmas, leaving our baby in intensive care, fighting for her life. You both thought it might cheer me up.

Driving into millionaires' row was like becoming part of a story in a Grimm's fairy tale. Mullioned glass and tall turrets were patchy with snow, I felt we had entered a child's picture book. The princess would surely call out Rapunzel-like from these castle windows. There were few people around, it was not the tourist season and the emptiness added to the magic.

There is Chateau-sur-mer, built by profit trading with China in the 1850s with the intricate Italian woodwork by Luigi Frullini of Florence and coloured glass skylights that fill the mansion with the colour of mother-of-pearl. The Elms on Bellvue Avenue is a copy of the Chateau d'Anciers near Paris. The grounds are manicured and full of bronze and marble statues, fountains, terraces and gazebos and eighteenth-century sunken formal gardens. Beauty, elegance, history and all I think of is why are there so many tourists on such a cold Spring day. I still do not feel like a tourist even after all these years, I still have a sense of ownership and pride that this place is part of Rhode Island and I used to live here. I think of the numbers of times we brought visitors to Newport, feeling and acting like a local. As tourists, they could not be part of it.

They didn't belong.

'You are a tourist. You don't live here any more.' Your voice was gentle and amused.

CHAPTER 25

The four of us drive to the lake. Will it be as beautiful? We turn into Ruffstone Road, past the beach, past Norma's place. Kitty and Mac's house seems somehow smaller, the lake somehow seems smaller. The Rhododendron bushes are bent after the unseasonal snow. Everything still looks bleak and battered after the unexpected, violent storm. Soon the Lily-of-the-Valley will be flowering. Hyacinths, tulips, daffodils are already beginning to flower and the buds on the Dogwood are ready to burst despite the unseasonal snow. They know that it is spring! I wonder if they are the bulbs I planted. I hope that they are.

Many of the aspen trees have been removed from around the lake.

Someone is living in the house, the lights are on, someone is moving around. You decide to knock on the door, the wolf's head knocker is still here. Someone has restained the door. Ben and Tilly get out of the car and decide to walk down the road towards the dead-end past Kitty and Macmillan's house (I can't think of anyone else living there; it will always be their house). I would have loved them to see Emma as a grown woman, so beautiful and competent. I look over at the large picture window and think of the number of times we crossed the road to chat and the number of times I saw her just standing there. A woman behind glass. I always wondered how she kept her windows so clean. They are not sparkling now, there is no one looking out, curious about these strangers in Ruffstone Road.

But it is the pontoon which draws me, and the trees, which used to be like a forest around the cottage. I listen for the quack of ducks. They would have returned by now. Do these people feed them and have names for them? I will be trespassing if I walk down to the water's edge, to the lake. So I stand by the edge of the drive, sloping down to the water, feeling shy and uncomfortable. I am no longer part of the rhythm of life in this place.

Someone comes to the door. I can see he is wearing a lumberjack shirt, is dark with a black moustache and thick black eyebrows. He leans against the door, comes out, looks at me standing looking at the pontoon. I am seeing things he can never imagine,

You are walking away after talking and laughing with him. He is going inside, closing the door.

'He's buying the house. They're going to make changes.' It is as if I have been slapped.

'He knew who we were. Said that he knew our names on the door in the linen cupboard, Lily and Peter Travis, Australia (you had added Emma's name when we brought her home from hospital the first time) and that that is something he will always keep. He didn't ask us in, although I kept hinting at it.'

I have a feeling of ending, but a good feeling of so many memories and pictures in my mind of the faces of people we loved. We lived rich lives in this beautiful place. Whatever changes anyone makes, we will always have that. Perhaps I am letting go.

Perhaps Emma will return again to the place of her birth and look at her reflection in the lake. Perhaps in her reflection she will see the past, hear a small child's voice whispering among the aspen trees.

My last memory of the cottage as we begin to drive away is the mailbox. Someone has painted two ducks in full flight across it.

The Author

Tess Driver lives between the sea and the scrub on the Fleurieu Peninsula in South Australia, after teaching and working in Australia, England, America and Asia. She has a BA in Asian History and an MA in Creative Writing from Adelaide University.

Her work has featured in librettos and in *My Love My Life*, an Adelaide Festival Opera. She edited *Jennifer*, written by Jeannie Forster Young for the Year of Women's Sufferance and her biography *Chord of Silk*, on the singer Rita Coonan. She was short listed for the Angus and Robertson Book Prize.

As a poet, she has many published collections in America, *The Best Poets in Australia* and *The Best Poets in Britain*.

The Lake is her first novel.